He's Back. . . .

Kirsten turned back to her work, shutting down the WXRJ sound booth, when the phone rang. *That's weird,* she thought. The tech studio wasn't supposed to send callers to the sound booth after the show ended. She looked at the digital readout, but there was no flashing caller ID number. The phone kept ringing. After a few more seconds of hesitation, she answered it. *"Love Stinks,"* she said in her best professional voice.

"I know," a guy replied.

Kirsten's hands began to shake. It sounded like . . . *him.* Like Kyle. But it couldn't be, right? It couldn't! "Caller, can you please identify yourself?" she asked.

"It's me, Kirsten," the voice said.

Kirsten almost fell out of her chair. It *was* Kyle. She'd recognize his deep, breathy voice anywhere. Just the very *sound* of it started to constrict her lungs. *This has to be a dream,* she told herself. *Another nightmare!*

"I need to speak to you," he said.

the
party
room

AFTER HOURS

MORGAN BURKE

SIMON PULSE

New York London Toronto Sydney

To Gwen Bond. You are the one.

〜 SIMON PULSE
An imprint of Simon & Schuster
Children's Publishing Division
1230 Avenue of the Americas, New York, NY 10020

SIMON PULSE and colophon are registered trademarks of Simon & Schuster, Inc.

A Parachute Press Book
Designed by Greg Stadnyk
The text of this book was set in Photina.
Manufactured in the United States of America
First Simon Pulse edition April 2005

10 9 8 7 6 5 4 3 2 1

Library of Congress Control Number 2004107478
ISBN 0-689-87226-7

Part One

Prologue

Don't worry. I haven't forgotten about you. No, not at all.

Your turn will come. . .

Oh, it hasn't been easy, this waiting. It takes a lot of patience and control.

And practice . . .

But my technique is perfect now.

Yes, you heard me. Killing Samantha Byrne and Emma Lewis was PRACTICE!

And it was fun.

I liked hearing them scream and beg. I LIKED IT!

I was almost sad when it was over. The lifeless look in their eyes. The blood running from their heads and out their mouths.

I thought wrapping Sam's hands with a Talcott tie was a nice touch, didn't you?

Oh. Of course you didn't.

I know, I know . . . so sad . . . so, so sad. . . .

But I'm coming for you. Do you hear me?

I want to see YOU gasp for air. I want to see YOU choke on your own blood. I want to be THE LAST THING YOU SEE when you take your final breath.

No, I won't let you get away.

It's time . . . IT'S TIME!

"I still see him,"

seventeen-year-old Kirsten Sawyer told her best friend, Julie Pembroke. She ran a shaky hand through her super-long chestnut-colored hair as she paced Julie's Victorian bedroom.

"Who?" Julie croaked from underneath a pile of covers on her bed.

"Kyle . . . I mean, Paul Stone . . . or whatever his name is," Kirsten said. She thought back to that day last October when she'd first met him and he'd told her his name was Kyle. He was so sweet and understanding when Kirsten told him how upset she was. That her best friend, Samantha Byrne, had been missing for days. Of course he was. It was later when Kirsten found out that Kyle was really Paul Stone, a convicted killer.

"You couldn't sleep again?" Julie asked.

Kirsten shook her head. "Every time I close my eyes, it's like he's on the inside of my eyelids. I even thought I saw him at the Party Room last weekend, Jules. It could have been him, right? He said he'd be back, remember?"

"Kirsten, think about it. There's *no way* he'd come back to the city. The police are looking for him big-time." Julie sat up in a sea of frilly designer sheets. Her hair was a mess of cropped blond bed-head, and two dark circles underneath her blue eyes were just waiting for some concealer. "Don't forget, he was convicted of killing Carolee Adams three years ago. And he's the major suspect in *two* new murder cases, Emma Lewis and—"

"Sam Byrne! I know!" Kirsten snapped. "How could I forget? She was our best friend! And she wound up dead in Central Park— practically right underneath my bedroom window. Kyle killed her. Wrapped her wrists in his Talcott tie before he bashed her head in and stabbed her and—"

"Stop it!" Julie cried. "This is sick. You can't keep reliving it. You know Sam wouldn't want that. Why can't you . . . just . . . stop?"

"How could we know what Sam would

have wanted?" Kirsten asked. And how could Julie expect her to ignore the pain? She pulled a well-worn snapshot out of her jeans pocket. *The Three Amigas*—Julie, Kirsten, and Sam—hugging each other on the front steps of their old high school in Riverdale, The Woodley School. It was taken on the first day of senior year. They looked so happy then. So excited about their future after high school, only . . . Sam didn't graduate, did she?

Now that high school was over and done with, Kirsten and Julie were going to spend the summer between Manhattan and Julie's house in the Hamptons before they began college in the fall.

Their other two friends, Sarah Goldstein and Carla Hernandez, had already left for a summer in Tuscany. Then they were off to college at Barnard for four years. Who knew if Kirsten would even see them again? That's how much things had changed.

It was weird. The five girls had been inseparable all through grammar school, junior high and high school. Through first dates and first drinks and first loves. But then Sam died. Now Kirsten and Julie were hardly friends with Carla and Sarah. They'd barely hugged at the Woodley graduation ceremony, and they only occasionally e-mailed one another.

They couldn't handle it anymore, Kirsten thought. *Carla and Sarah wanted to forget what Sam went through—and they did.*

"Just try to relax a little, okay?" Julie said.

"It's useless," Kirsten muttered, shoving the photo into the pocket of her Coach tote bag. She glanced out the window. "Plus it's late." Last night they had stayed out until ten . . . in the morning. Then she'd spent the rest of the day tossing and turning in Julie's bed. Now it was night again. It was time to go out—or maybe even go home.

"After the party, there's the after-party," Julie sang groggily, and made a goofy face at Kirsten, but Kirsten didn't smile.

"I've got to go, Jules," she said, suddenly feeling claustrophobic in the enormous room. "I'll call you later, okay?" she said, grabbing her pink Coach tote and slipping into her matching Manolos. She opened the large oak door that led to the rest of Julie's sprawling town house.

"Wait, Kirsten!" Julie said. "Why don't you

just stay over? I'll have the cook make us something sinful and we can have a movie marathon or something."

But Kirsten hurried out of the room. Out of the house. Out onto the hot, blustering street, the hot, balmy June air coating her arms and neck as she walked down Eighty-fourth Street on the Upper East Side of Manhattan.

It was dark outside, and Kirsten couldn't believe she had wasted an entire day in freak-out mode. *It's ridiculous*, she thought. *Maybe Julie is right.* She glanced at her watch, but the face was blurry. She blinked. *Last night was rough, but I didn't think it was* that *rough.*

A garbage can lid clattered to the sidewalk behind Kirsten, and she whipped around. Nothing there.

Of course there's nothing there, Kirsten scolded herself. *Stop being so jumpy. Stop thinking people are out to get you. Just stop it!*

But still, every house seemed foreboding—every alleyway dark and scary.

New York isn't my city anymore, she thought as she hustled down the empty street. Her home hadn't been the same place ever since the last time she saw Kyle—the night he tried to kill her, and she'd escaped. Kirsten used to love the vastness of Manhattan; it felt like a big, anonymous playground. But now each stairwell, each unknown intersection, each shady building was just another hiding place for a murderer.

"Come inside, baaaa-bbbby."

Kirsten gasped and spun around again to see an elderly woman coaxing an overgrown shih tzu into a Bentley.

"Stupid, Kirsten," she muttered, resolving to make it home without suffering another breakdown. She hugged herself as she hurried down Eighty-fourth Street, nearing Lexington. Then, unmistakably loud and clear, Kirsten heard heavy footsteps start off on the pavement behind her. She glanced back, spotting a scruffy older man with graying hair across the street.

As nonchalant as Kirsten tried to be, she could feel the muscles in her neck contract. *Calm down, freak show. He's across the street— besides, people are allowed to walk around at night*, she told herself, but her stomach began to tighten as the man suddenly crossed to her side of the street. His footsteps quickened.

So did Kirsten's. What if it *wasn't* all in her head? She tucked her purse under her arm and started hustling around the corner of Eighty-fourth and Lexington. Tearing across the street, she headed uptown, toward a busier Eighty-sixth Street, instead of heading to her building, which was on Eighty-first and Fifth. There was a subway there, and shops.

The footsteps kept coming as Kirsten raced toward the entrance. He was getting closer! Swerving through Eighty-sixth Street's traffic, barely dodging a crosstown bus, Kirsten booked across the street. There was nowhere to go except down into the subway station.

Taking three steps at a time, she stumbled down the urine-soaked stairwell, falling to her knees.

"Owww!" A shock of pain ran up Kirsten's leg. A deep cut crisscrossed her knee. Then Kirsten saw her pursuer bounding down the stairs! She jumped up and darted toward the platform entrance and hopped the turnstile, ignoring the shouts of a Jamaican token-booth operator behind her. She hopped onto a local train just as the doors were slamming shut.

Finally safe, Kirsten stared at the man through the train's scratched-up window. He was running toward another woman on the platform now. When he reached her, he gave her an enormous hug and a kiss on the cheek. *Oh, my God. He was rushing to meet his girlfriend or wife or something,*

She felt like a total idiot. Again.

"What the hell is wrong with me?" Kirsten muttered as the train screeched out of the station. She collapsed onto a gray bench and caught her breath, each gasp stinging her overworked lungs. She glanced around the empty subway car. *Not a good thing,* she thought.

Kirsten stood up again and decided to move to the next car, where she hoped she would see some people. But as she pulled open the metal door at the end of the car and walked into the next one, the overhead light flickered, then went black. A high-pitched sound of metal grinding on metal pierced her ears, and the train suddenly stopped, tossing Kirsten into the next car.

Someone must've pulled the emergency brake, Kirsten thought. She felt her way in the dark for a bench to sit on to wait for the conductor's announcement. Clearly there was no one in this car either.

Her arms outstretched, she turned and slipped on something, falling to the ground. The floor was slick for some reason. Wet. Sticky. And there was a stale metallic smell in the air. She tried to pull herself up, reaching blindly for a door handle, when the lights came back on.

Kirsten gasped. She was sitting in a pool of blood! Thick, gooey redness seeped into the fabric of her skirt. Hands and legs were slick and shiny and red. Slathered with blood. Covered with blood!

"I *told* you I was coming back," a voice said.

Kirsten looked up. Kyle, wide-eyed and manic, stood at the other end of the subway car! Kirsten tried to scream, but nothing came out of her throat.

Kyle walked slowly toward her, holding out a bloodstained tie. A *Talcott* tie! "I've come for you, Kirsten," he said, "just for you . . ."

The lights dimmed as Kyle broke into a run, his eyes piercing her mind, paralyzing her limbs.

"Save me!" Kirsten screamed. "Someone save me!"

9

2

"Save me," Kirsten said
again, and opened her eyes.

She was lying on a black leather reclining chair in an ultramodern Midtown office. No books. No warm pillows to cry into. Just a lone Calder print looming on the wall, herself in that chair and a concerned Dr. Helen Fitzgerald, Psychiatrist, staring at her from across the room. Somewhere, water was straining through a Zen rock garden.

"And then I woke up," Kirsten added. "Just like last time. The dream is always the same. It starts off with a normal conversation about Sam, and then it gets freaky and I end up covered in blood. Just before something really awful happens, I wake up," she sighed, not bothering to make eye contact with her newest psychiatrist.

. "And then you can't fall back to sleep," Dr. Fitzgerald said.

Kirsten rolled her eyes. "Ding, ding, ding! Ten points for the psychiatrist in the blue suit."

Dr. Fitzgerald stiffened in her chair and smoothed a strand of short brown hair in place. She was Kirsten's third psychiatrist in as many months. *What's she going to say or do that's any different?* Kirsten thought as she looked the woman over.

Kirsten had already made a string of assumptions about her newest doctor: Fitzgerald was a forty-ish spinster whose Moderne taste was merely a cover-up for an ultra-boring lifestyle. She probably lived with fifteen cats and hoarded price-saver coupons.

"You've got to have patience, Kirsten," Fitzgerald assured her.

"But when am I going to stop freaking out over *nothing*?" Kirsten replied. "I mean, every minute of every day? Come on. And don't give me that psychobabble about having post-traumatic stress disorder. That doesn't help me."

"You've been through a lot." Fitzgerald crossed her legs and stared into Kirsten's eyes.

"Don't deny yourself that. Don't try to speed through some quick-fix recovery."

"A quick fix is *exactly* what I need!" Kirsten yelled, though not really meaning it. She could be a bitch when she wanted to.

"That's bullshit, Kirsten, and you know it," Fitzgerald snapped back. "Stop hiding from the *real* issues."

Whoa. Hello. Kirsten jerked into a sitting position. *Maybe this one isn't like the others.*

"I'm here to help you," Dr. Fitzgerald added in a softer tone. "I'm not going to sit here and watch you suffer."

"I . . . feel . . . so . . . *guilty*," Kirsten heard herself confess. Her voice didn't even sound like her own. It was high-pitched and tentative, like a little girl's voice. She felt nervous sharing this deeper thought, but somehow, Fitzgerald's blunt honesty had made her seem trustworthy.

"How so?" Fitzgerald asked. Attentive. Clear. *Interested.*

No one wanted to hear about Kirsten's stresses anymore. She was a broken record. A record most of her friends and family wanted to store in the attic and forget all about. Even

Kirsten was tired of going over the same memories—it had to stop. But how?

Fitzgerald stared into Kirsten's eyes with a warm, inviting smile that said, "It's okay. . . ."

"I can't help thinking that if I hadn't lied to Sam's parents and the police about where Sam was the night she vanished, maybe they could've found her in time. Before Kyle got to her," Kirsten admitted. "And . . . maybe if I had never met Kyle . . . or never attended Woodley . . . or never *existed,* maybe Emma would still be alive too!" Kirsten stared at Fitzgerald, tears streaming from her eyes. "It's *my* fault they're dead . . . *my* fault!" Kirsten sucked in a deep breath and went silent, clasping her shaking hands and waiting for the doctor to say something.

But she didn't—not for a while.

"Well, Kirsten," Fitzgerald finally began. "In psychiatric terms, when someone follows you in your dream world, it usually means that you're actually *looking* for someone. To save you. Because—"

"You are everyone in your dreams," Kirsten finished her sentence. "Freud."

"Ding, ding, ding! Ten points for the

woman in the five-hundred-dollar shoes." Dr. Fitzgerald cracked a smile.

Fitzgerald definitely didn't have fifteen cats, Kirsten decided. "Sorry," she said. "I just want to be normal, you know?"

"And you deserve to find that normalcy," Fitzgerald replied. "You've been through hell and back, and now it's time to regroup. To regain the power over your life, to get some strength."

"Or just some *rest*," Kirsten added. "I'd be happy with just one good night of sleep."

"This should help a little," Fitzgerald told Kirsten as she scribbled out a prescription. "Just don't take more than one sleeping pill per night."

"Thanks." Kirsten smiled.

"But more than anything, Kirsten, the only way for you to feel better is to stay busy. Stay positive."

"Easier said than done," Kirsten replied.

"Well, for starters, your mom told me that you're working at a radio station this summer. WXRJ?"

"*Interning,*" Kirsten corrected her.

"Pay or no pay, it's a great way to start

dealing with life. Healthy distractions can offer a positive way to deal with loss."

"I guess you're right," Kirsten said. "If I keep obsessing over the past, why would the present get any better?"

"Exactly!" Fitzgerald smiled as she handed Kirsten the small white prescription note.

Kirsten tucked it into her purse.

And with that, Fitzgerald closed her notebook and stood up. "It's time to start your new life, Kirsten. It's time to move on."

3

"I don't get it," a male voice said from across the phone line.

"Because once you love *yourself* and really understand *why* you are interesting and unique, Maury, then you'll feel confident dating other people," Kate Grisholm replied.

"Ohhh, *now* I get it," Maury said.

Kirsten cracked a smile as she watched her boss give advice to a caller on her radio show. Two weeks into her internship at WXRJ and Kirsten was already fielding calls and monitoring the radio feed from where she worked in a room with computers they called the tech room. She knew working on *Love Stinks, with Kate Grisholm* would be interesting, but she'd had no idea that she'd be doing so much with the live show. She loved the sense of responsibility her job gave her.

Out in Studio Five, Kate gave Kirsten a

thumbs-up sign and transferred the call back to Kirsten.

"Thanks for calling *Love Stinks,*" Kirsten added before letting the caller go.

"No—thank *you,*" he replied. "From now on, I'm gonna say, 'Maury, you're the man!'"

"Exactly! You're the man, Maury!" Kirsten hung up and laughed to herself.

"What's so funny?" a guy behind her asked.

Kirsten gasped, startled. She spun around in her seat—to see a total hottie looking out from a tangle of blond hair and holding a stack of manila envelopes.

"Whoa. Sorry. I didn't mean to scare you." The hottie smiled. Cute.

"You didn't *scare* me," Kirsten lied, trying to regain her cool factor, which was not going to be easy.

"I'm Brian."

"Kirsten."

An awkward pause.

"I'm a mail," Brian stated proudly, breaking the silence.

"I can see that." Kirsten smirked. Okay, maybe seeming cool to this guy would be easier than she'd thought.

"Oh . . . no, um, I'm a *mail intern* is what I meant to say," Brian added, nodding at the envelopes in his hands with a shy grin. "Today's my first day."

"I can see that too," Kirsten couldn't help teasing him.

Brian's face flushed. He was cute. Very cute.

"I mean, in a perfect world, I'd be down in Cape May surfing or whatever," Brian loosened up, leaning against the doorway. "But as far as work goes, radio's pretty cool, you know?"

"So you're not from the city?" Kirsten asked, even though it was obvious that he wasn't. He had "I'm-not-from-Manhattan" written all over him. Wild and wavy blond hair, extremely loose Ocean Pacific pants, and granola-boy sandals. She liked it.

"Me? No way. I'm from New Jersey." Brian chuckled and looked at his feet.

"Well, I'd be happy to show you the ropes, Jersey Boy." Kirsten winked and looked him over again. He seemed nice. Different. It was refreshing to talk to a guy who was a little shy—not like the guys she was used to being around.

18

"Really? That'd be great because—"

Just then, Kirsten noticed Kate Grisholm taking off her headphones and closing down the main studio. The show was ending.

"Shit!" Kirsten shouted. She turned back to the phones, transferring the waiting calls to the sign-off tape that told them to call tomorrow, "even if Love Stinks!" Kate was a tough boss who expected everything to run like clockwork, and Kirsten didn't want to mess up this opportunity. "Earth to Kirsten," Kirsten joked, turning back to Brian. "I totally spaced out for a second. . . . Long weekend."

"That's cool." Brian grinned as he tucked a ringlet behind his ear. "I space out all the time."

"Really?"

"Mmm-hmm . . . ," Brian said.

Again, silence butted its way into their conversation. This time, however, it was kind of sweet.

"Well, it's very nice to meet you, Kirsten," Brian said finally.

Back out in the main studio, Kate rapped against the glass partition and mouthed *good night* to her interns.

19

"Oops," Kirsten said, jumping up to clear out the studio before the next show.

"Oh. I'm getting you in trouble," Brian realized. "Let me get out of your way. . . . Um . . . okay, then . . ." Brian frowned slightly, shrugged his shoulders, and walked out.

"Wait. Brian?" Kirsten looked up, realizing she might have seemed a little rude, but Brian was already halfway down the hallway with his pile of mail. "See you around!" she called out, trying to salvage her first interaction with the only cute guy her age at WXRJ.

Kirsten turned back to her work, straightening Studio Five WXRJ, when the phone rang. *That's weird,* she thought. *The calls aren't supposed to come into the studio after the show's ended.* She looked at the digital readout, but there was no flashing caller ID number. The phone kept ringing. After a few more seconds of hesitation, she answered it. *"Love Stinks,"* she said in her best professional voice.

"I know," a guy replied.

Kirsten's hands began to shake. It sounded like . . . *him.* Like Kyle. But it couldn't be, right?

It couldn't! "Caller, can you please identify yourself?" she asked.

"It's me, Kirsten," the voice said.

Kirsten almost fell out of her chair. It *was* Kyle. She'd recognize his deep, breathy voice anywhere. Just the very *sound* of it started to constrict her lungs. *This has to be a dream,* she told herself. *Another nightmare!*

"I need to speak to you," he said. His voice sounded urgent, upset.

"How did you know where to find me?" she asked him, starting to panic, wondering *where* he was calling from. Was he back in New York? Could he have gotten in the station somehow?

"I—I just want to talk," he said.

Frightened, Kirsten looked around for Brian. Maybe she could get him—or anybody—to walk her out of the building. But Brian was gone, and the studio seemed strangely quiet.

"How did you get this number?" Kirsten demanded again.

"I couldn't risk calling your cell," Kyle explained. "I found out where you were through Woodley's intern program."

Kirsten felt her stomach flood with acid. Not even one of the most prestigious schools in the country could protect her privacy. "Leave me alone, Kyle, I mean, *Paul*!" she screamed, and grabbed her purse off a desk.

"Don't use that name!" he yelled back. "And I told you. I just want to talk. You don't have to be afraid of me!"

Yeah, right. That's what he said the last time I saw him—right before he tried to kill me! Kirsten slammed her headset on the desk and bolted out of the studio, knocking over a stack of DAT tapes on her way out.

As Kirsten fumbled with the keys to Studio Five, she heard a door open somewhere down the hallway; she shuddered with desperation. She found the right key, jammed it into the lock, and booked it down the long hallway. She'd make it to security on the first floor and stay there all night if she had to.

Kirsten rounded the corner and slammed into a waiting elevator. She must've pressed "L" a hundred times as she waited for the door to close. *Almost there, almost there . . .*

Then, just as the brass door began to

swish closed, a hand slipped through the opening!

It's him! Kirsten thought, squeezing here eyes shut. *He said he'd come back for me—and here he is!*

4

"Where are you rushing off to?" Kate asked, shifting her large leather bag onto her shoulder.

Kirsten opened her eyes as the elevator door closed. She was now alone with her boss for the first time and she was acting like a crazy person!

"Are you all right?" Kate asked.

"Oh . . . I, uh . . . I have an appointment," Kirsten said, trying to come up with something believable. "A doctor's appointment." A line of sweat beaded across her forehead.

Kate frowned. "At night?" she asked. The lie wasn't very good.

"What?" Kirsten said, racking her brain for a better excuse. Nothing.

"You have an appointment *at night*? You must have a great doctor," Kate added.

"Yep. It's part of a new health plan at

Sinai," Kirsten said as they arrived at the lobby and the elevator door opened. "See you tomorrow!" She bolted out of the elevator and through the main lobby.

As Kirsten ran into the pedestrian traffic of Times Square, thoughts of Kyle slammed back into her head. She looked around frantically, trying to find him in a sea of faces, but Times Square was too bright and too busy. A garish electronic billboard flashed obnoxiously on the side of a building, illuminating the people with shades of greens, blues, browns. *Kyle could be anywhere!*

Kirsten pushed her way up Broadway, but she had no idea where she was headed. Her parents were off antiquing upstate somewhere and wouldn't get back until tomorrow. And Kirsten didn't exactly want to go home to an empty apartment right about now. Then she realized there was only one place she wanted to be at a time like this—one place where she'd feel safe, at least for a little while.

Kirsten rooted through her purse, found her cell phone, and punched in a number as she jostled through the people and made her way toward the Upper East Side of

Manhattan. One ring, two rings, three rings . . .

Come on. Come on! Kirsten thought.

"What's up, baby?" Julie answered.

"Meet me at the Party Room!" Kirsten said.

"Sounds like you handled it well," Scott, the infamous bartender at the Party Room, yelled over a pack of giggling Woodley School sophomores as he handed Kirsten one of his trademark mojitos.

The Party Room's elegant oak bar was packed tonight, with the usual crowd of soon-to-be power players in the business world, fashion world, publishing world . . . or *any* world they wanted, really. In other words, an elite group that defined what it meant to be young and rich in New York City, *and* who knew how to work it. Oh, there were a few faces missing, probably already summering in Provence or wherever their families liked to summer. Others, like Kirsten, were biding their time in the city, working at amazingly fortunate internships and making the trek out to their family's twenty-eight-room summer "cottages" in the Hamptons on Long Island every Friday night.

"Come on, Scott," Kirsten said. "I broke out into a cold sweat and Kate *knew* I was lying. It wasn't pretty, believe me! Now my boss is *sure* I'm a lunatic".

"Well, so what?" Scott said. "You had a right to freak out. You got a call from a *murderer.* Give me a break!"

"Yeah, about that call . . . ," Kirsten began. "I was so *sure* it was Kyle, but now . . . I don't know. Maybe I was just imagining it. Maybe I just freaked out again." She took a long sip of her drink, suddenly feeling exhausted from the whole ordeal.

Scott ignored the b-boy who was standing at the bar, waiting for a refill of Guinness, and rested a brotherly hand on Kirsten's arm. "You're going to be okay," he said, "but I don't want you to be taking any chances with this guy. He's a maniac. If you think he called you, I believe you, Kirsten. Don't doubt your instincts."

"Thanks, Scott-land," Kirsten said. Over the past few months he had become a real friend. When most of her other friends had begun to doubt Kirsten's sanity, Scott had always been there to support her, making her feel comfortable and safe. She didn't know what she'd do without him.

"And don't worry about the elevator thing with your boss," Scott continued. "Kate Grisholm probably didn't even notice it."

Forever busy, Scott turned to help the giggling girls and the b-boy. The sophomores ordered their requisite draft beers and when Scott leaned over to get some glasses, they literally gasped at the view of what could quite possibly be the world's most perfect ass.

Desperate much? Kirsten thought. Giggly sophomores were so hilarious, but she couldn't blame them, really. Scott was a major hottie, for sure—kind of like a young Tom-Cruise-meets-Justin-Timberlake type, only taller and nicer and with a smile that could melt a heart from a thousand miles away.

Kirsten smiled for a moment. She and her friends had been just like that back in tenth grade. To them, every night they were able to get into The Party Room was another night they'd spent leaning up against the bar, licking their lips as seductively as they could, angling to score some free drinks from the hot bartender.

Kirsten laughed out loud. She felt a rush of alcohol swirl in her brain, so she steadied herself on her barstool.

"What's so funny?" someone asked.

Kirsten smiled and spun around. "Jules! I'm so glad to see you!" She immediately sprang forward and hugged her. As she squeezed Julie tight, Kirsten felt a swelling in her throat, the kind that promised tears.

"Um, good to see you too," Julie said. "What's up, Kirsten?"

"I just really need a friend right now. I—I think he called me today," Kirsten confessed, pulling back.

"Who?" Julie clearly had no idea why Kirsten dragged her out tonight.

"Kyle!" Kirsten cried. "Who else?"

Julie rolled her eyes. "Oh."

Kirsten tilted her head. What was that all about? Then she realized. "Oh, my God," she murmured. "Not you, too, Jules. . . . You don't believe me!"

"No, sweetie . . . sure, I do . . ." Julie paused. "Well, at least I *want* to. It's just that there've been so many times when—"

"When *what?*" Kirsten demanded. She was

getting angry now. Sure, it was okay if Kirsten doubted herself at times, but Julie was her *best friend;* someone who was supposed to be there—through good times and bad.

"Nothing. Forget it," Julie said. She sat at the bar, and Scott poured her her usual pomegranate martini.

But Kirsten wasn't finished. She wanted to know what Julie was really thinking. "Say it, Julie!"

"Okay!" Julie shrugged. "It's just that you've been kind of . . . extra *sensitive* lately . . . and . . . um . . . I'm not sure when you're experiencing something real or just *thinking* it's real." Julie put a hand on Kirsten's shoulder. "Like the other day, for instance. Remember when you thought someone was chasing you and it turned out to be just some guy rushing to meet his wife?"

Kirsten nodded. The comment hit her like a punch . . . because it was true.

"I mean, how do you know it was Kyle?" she asked. "Did he say, 'Hi, it's Kyle'?"

Kirsten thought back. "No, not exactly," she admitted. Did she freak out over nothing again? Did Kyle really call her, or was it all in her head? Her head began to swirl, thinking about it all.

Julie sighed and looked at the bar. "Look, I didn't mean to—"

"No." Kirsten sighed. "You're right." She stared into Julie's eyes. "I'm losing it."

And this time, Julie hugged her back. They embraced for a long time at the bar as people looked on.

"That's what friends are for!" sang a sarcastic voice behind Kirsten and Julie.

The two girls simultaneously turned around to find themselves face-to-face with Leslie Fenk, otherwise known as the Woodley Bitch.

"You guys gonna get out of the way or what?" Leslie slurred.

Julie smirked at Leslie's slutty Gaultier dress. With her platinum-highlighted hair pulled into a messy-on-purpose ponytail, Leslie looked like a bad version of Nicole Richie tonight. "Take *my* seat. All of a sudden I feel sick." Julie hopped off her stool and leaned into Kirsten's ear. "Gotta go to the bathroom," she whispered. "Hold Leslie off until I get back."

Kirsten laughed as Julie hurried off through the crowded bar.

Leslie tilted her head. "Do you have something to share with the rest of the class, Ms. Sawyer?" she quipped sarcastically.

"You know what, Leslie?" Kirsten sighed. "I'm not in the mood today." She drained her glass and tried to get Scott's attention. He was swamped, so she'd have to suffer through more alone time with Leslie until Julie returned.

"What happened to poor little Kirrrrrrsten *this* time?" Leslie pressed, swaying back and forth. She was loaded.

"Life happened," Kirsten found herself saying.

"Amen to that, sister," Leslie slurred heavily as she plopped down on the stool next to Kirsten.

"SISTER"? Did Leslie Fenk just call me "sister"? The night was getting weirder and weirder. The two rivals sat quietly for a moment as they both strained to get Scott's attention.

"Know why everyone thinks I'm such a bitch?" Leslie suddenly asked, making sure her neckline plunged deep enough for Scott.

"I don't know." Kirsten rolled her eyes. "Why?"

Leslie laughed to herself and then faced Kirsten with a smile. "'Cause I am!" she cheered. Leslie was in rare form tonight.

As hard as she tried to remain icy, Kirsten felt a smile creep across her own face.

"I just can't help it," Leslie added. "It's like people with Tourette's syndrome, or whatever it's called. They bark out all this weird stuff every now and then, even if they don't want to, even though they *wanna* bottle up all that stuff and just . . . be . . . normal and nice-y, nice. . . . I mean, if someone's wearing double denim or has a reeaallly vicious panty line or something like that," Leslie continued, "it's only so long before I have to say *something* about it, right? Like, 'Howdy buckaroo!' Or, 'Are you wearing Depends?'"

Kirsten broke into a laugh. *At least Leslie is funny. I could use some comic relief.*

"Do I make any sense at all?" Leslie asked as she leaned into the brass railing that lined the bar. She was cashing out. Big-time.

"Maybe." Kirsten shrugged.

"Hey, pep up!" Leslie said, poking Kirsten in the arm several times. "I feel like I'm talking to a brick wall."

Kirsten rolled her eyes. "Sorry to disappoint you, Leslie, but I *told* you I'm not in the mood for fun and games."

"Okaaaaay, okaaaaay," Leslie said, holding up her hands. Then she let out a big, exaggerated sigh and opened her tiny leopard Gucci party purse. "Look, I was going to save this for myself, but *obviously* you need it more than I do." She pulled out something and shoved it into Kirsten's palm. "Don't say I never gave you anything."

Kirsten looked at the two iridescent green pills in her hand.

"A little pick-me-up!" Leslie said. "Go for it." And with that, she slid off the barstool, kissed Kirsten on both cheeks, and slunk off to a posse of frat boys.

Did that just happen? Kirsten asked herself as she watched Leslie flirt. Then she glanced at the pills. *I've been a real drag lately. Maybe I do need a little help.*

Julie returned from the bathroom. "So did you tell her off?" she asked Kirsten.

Kirsten discretely downed the pills and chased them with Julie's drink. Then she turned to face her friend. "Totally," she lied.

Julie sat back down and slung an arm over Kirsten's shoulder. "Let's just forget about Kyle altogether tonight, all right?"

"You're right," Kirsten agreed. "I don't want to think about him ever again."

5

Think it's that easy? Think you can just snap your fingers and wish me away?

I hate this place. Too hot in the summer. Stinks like urine, rotting garbage, horse crap.

It blows my mind how naive you can be.

You can't run away from me.

I'm just growing stronger. Smarter. Bolder. All the time keeping my control, though.

I won't give you the satisfaction of losing my temper again. Everything I do is cool. Cold. Frosty, even.

You see, I'm whistling while I work!

Hot, hot heat. It's boiling inside. Shit!

You WON'T slip away this time! You can't HIDE FROM YOUR FATE!

You've just been lucky. That's all. But luck changes just like everything else. Just like you've changed. Just like my life changed when you entered it.

Well, now it's time to leave my life. Get out for good.

YOU GOT THAT!?

Too hot.

Can't breathe.

Got . . . to . . . breathe. That's all. Just . . . find . . . some . . . space.

It's only a matter of time.

And I've got all the time in the world. . . .

6

"See you next time!"
Kirsten hugged Scott as she stumbled out of
the Party Room.

Her friend was closing up inside, and the
smell of stale beer drove Kirsten to the street.
Scott had let her stick around until she was
the last person standing in the bar. Or almost
standing, as the case may be.

Julie was long gone already. Kirsten
vaguely remembered her friend leaving the
bar around midnight. Something about how
she'd rather watch *Sex and the City* reruns in
her town house than be "the latest cautionary
tale of 'debutantes gone bad.'"

Now what? Kirsten wondered. She was a little
drunk, but so totally awake, and she still didn't
feel like going home. But what else was there to
do? She stepped off the curb and jutted a hand
into the air to flag down a taxi.

An enormous stretch Hummer screeched along side, almost hitting her. "What the hell!" she cried, stumbling back onto the sidewalk. "You almost ran me over!"

Leslie Fenk popped her head out of the sunroof, grasping a glass of champagne. "Nice ass!" she cried, checking out Kirsten.

Kirsten snapped up and smoothed out the back of her miniskirt. "That's sexual harassment, Fenk!" Kirsten joked. "I'm getting a lawyer!"

"Ohh, I'm sooooo scared," Leslie played along.

"What's up?" Kirsten shouted as the Hummer idled loudly next to her.

"See for yourself." Leslie let out a low, trucker-size burp. "Get your butt in here!" she added before a hand reached up and pulled her down inside the car. Leslie screamed and laughed, then popped her head back out of the sunroof. "There's a hot deejay spinning at Vinyl tonight."

"You mean *this morning*?" Kirsten said.

"Yeah. Now. Whatever." Leslie apparently wasn't much for details. "He's got some kind of French name, so you know it's going to be tight. You coming?"

The door to the car opened, and Kirsten could hear the loud thumping of a vicious techno song. *Why not?* she thought. "Move over!" she said, and climbed into the car. As she slid into a plush leather seat, she was literally enveloped by a cloud of pot smoke. A crew of bug-eyed, chuckling Talcott boys were getting stoned as Leslie Fenk lay across their laps.

A kid in a black hoodie—red eyes peering out—shoved a short brown blunt in Kirsten's direction. Without even thinking, Kirsten took a long drag.

"Damn, Leslie!" one of the boys shouted. "You got more hot friends like this?"

The kid gave Kirsten a sinister smile, but she didn't care. She took another long drag, letting the pot smoke sting her lungs. As she coughed out smoke to the delight of the other bombed-out passengers, the Hummer screeched back to life and tore downtown.

Two songs later and the Hummer skidded to a halt outside the front doors of Vinyl. Kirsten and the rest of the crew poured out onto the street, laughing and shouting. Immediately, Leslie worked her flirtatious magic with a thick bouncer outside the club.

Within seconds, Kirsten found herself being swept up inside the velvet curtains.

The club was hot. Very hot. Break beats clacked through a vast, deep blue room.

Kirsten couldn't make out any faces yet— but she didn't have to. She knew who was there. Vinyl's regulars were a crazy mix of hip-hop heads from private schools, NYU kids on E, and strung-out performance artists from Williamsburg, Brooklyn.

Leslie's posse spread out into the jamming crowd, and Kirsten fought her way to the bar. "Anything strong!" she shouted to a sexy bartender over a pulsing Jungle track.

A shaky hand slapped a twenty down on the marble bar next to her. "It's on me."

Kirsten turned around to see Brandon Yardley, another recent Woodley graduate, looking, well, terrible: half-moons under his full-moon pupils, a ratty beard, his nostrils red and raw. It looked as if he'd been through hell and hadn't quite made it back yet.

Kirsten was definitely not in the mood to talk to him. He used to go out with Sam—and recently he'd gone from being a heavy drug user to a *really* heavy drug user. He was obnoxious and very aggressive, so much that he threatened Kirsten on several occasions after Sam's death. Now, looking at him wobbling and blinking, trying to make his eyes look "not so bloodshot," Kirsten never understood what Sam ever saw in him. Actually, she never understood it back then either.

Brandon stared at Kirsten for a long time, as if he was waiting for something.

"You look like a million bucks, Brandon," Kirsten finally cracked. She took a sip of a purplish concoction as the bartender made change for Brandon.

"Funny." Brandon's dead expression didn't change. "You don't look so hot yourself, Kirsten."

Good point.

"Thanks for the drink," Kirsten muttered, shaking her head and turning away.

"Wait. I want to tell you something. Something about Sam." Brandon grabbed her arm, stopping her.

"Just don't, Brandon," Kirsten warned. The last thing she wanted to do was talk to him about Sam. She remembered the last time he had gotten her alone and wanted to talk about Sam. It was on the last day she had seen Sam alive—after a late night at the Party Room. Sam had left early with some guy, and Brandon was jealous. In fact, he'd practically accosted Kirsten on the street, wanting to know where they were so that he could bash the guy's face in!

Then Kirsten noticed tears welling in Brandon's eyes. He let go of her arm and swiped them away. "Remember when we were all friends? You . . . me . . . Sam?" he asked. "You remember that, don't you? When everything was good?"

Kirsten nodded. She vaguely remembered a couple of times when they had all gone out together. It was fun. But that was before Sam broke up with him. Way before.

"I miss those times," he said. "You and I . . . we should be . . . I don't know . . . *friends*," Brandon added as he brushed a curl out of Kirsten's face. "*Close* friends. Don't you think Sam would have wanted that?"

"NO!" Kirsten cried. "You must be tripping on something serious tonight." She tried to move away from him, but Brandon stopped her.

"Listen to me for a second!" he yelled. "We

both lost Sam. And I lost Emma, too! I'm messed up, and I need to talk to someone. Is that so much to ask?"

Kirsten felt the tears coming back too. Why couldn't she get away from the pain for one night? Just one night! Kirsten pushed past Brandon, but he reeled her back in with no thought to his strength versus her slight frame.

"I know things, Kirsten!" he said, his eyes drugged out and wild. "You have to listen to me! I went to Talcott. I—"

"I can't do this, Brandon!" Kirsten winced. She could smell the whiskey on his breath. "No more! Please!"

Suddenly, Brandon's expression darkened. "Maybe you're right, Kirsten. I guess we can't be friends." His fingers crept slowly across Kirsten's chest, up her neck, around her throat.

"Get. Your. Hands. Off. Me," Kirsten said through clenched teeth. She reached down into her pocketbook and slowly found her keys, ready to stab. No one around them seemed to notice or care about their standoff. *You have no idea, Brandon,* she thought, feeling the rage swelling in her chest. She was tired of being a victim.

Brandon leaned into Kirsten, but right before she was forced to fight back, Leslie Fenk came to the rescue.

"Kirsten's *my* date tonight, Brannnndon!" Leslie chirped, nuzzling her cheek next to Kirsten's.

Brandon stepped away, shocked.

Kirsten relaxed, and added on to Leslie's game. "You didn't know about us, Brannnndon?"

"Whatever," Brandon slurred. "I'll get you later, Kirsten."

"Good luck, asshole!" Leslie shouted. "She's all mine!"

Although Leslie was quite possibly the craziest person Kirsten had ever met, at that moment, crazy seemed like the only way to be. Before her mother's voice could find its way over the thumping bass lines, Kirsten leaned over and kissed Leslie fully on the lips. "Thanks, Leslie. You saved my life."

"Woodley sluts unite!" Leslie screamed, and dragged her new pal toward the crowded dance floor.

As they fled, Kirsten managed to swing her head back to see Brandon one last time before a couple of girls dressed in vintage 1960s minidresses and rocking out to their own tune blocked her view.

The girls continued toward the dance floor, and Leslie handed Kirsten a small red pill with an "xxx" stamped on both sides. "Here," she said. "We're going to be here all night." Leslie swallowed an identical one and then twirled into the crowd with her hands in the air. "Now let's party!" she cried.

Kirsten swallowed hers and joined Leslie. As she let her body free, a flash of strobe lights went off through the club and the room started filling with white smoke. It rolled in thick, and soon Kirsten couldn't see anything around her.

Leslie squealed with joy as multicolored lasers pulsed through the smoke. "This is so crazy!"

A few minutes later, Kirsten began to feel a little woozy. She reached out for Leslie but couldn't find her anywhere. A cold gust raised the hair on the back of her neck, and Kirsten realized that she was alone.

In the center of a crowded, pulsing club, but completely alone.

7

BEEP! BEEP! BEEP! BEEP!
BEEP! BEE—

THWACK! Kirsten slammed her fist against her Hello Kitty alarm clock, knocking it to the floor. "Shit! I'm late!" she cried out. She blinked several times, but the bleary pain in her eyes wasn't going anywhere.

When she sat up in bed, Kirsten's head split open with pain. A series of images flashed through her mind: crashing on a couch in a back room of the club, someone strong dragging her back into the Hummer, a bumpy ride, more smoke filling her lungs, stumbling past José, her morning doorman.

Kirsten looked down at the alarm clock, still wailing on the floor.

12:16!

She was late. Very late. After the elevator run-in yesterday, Kirsten knew she couldn't afford to make another bad impression on Kate Grisholm.

She downed two of the pills Leslie had given her this morning and swallowed a lipstick-y glass of stale water, then scrambled to get dressed. No time for a shower. No time to worry about looking cute for that surfer boy, Brian.

No time to care, Kirsten reminded herself, and sprinted out of the apartment, down onto the street.

Summer in NYC was oppressive. It was already steamy outside when Kirsten raced out of the lobby. She broke into an immediate sweat as José hailed her a cab.

"You all right, Ms. Sawyer?" Jose asked.

"I'm fine, José, thanks," Kirsten blurted, sopping up the stream of sweat running down her back.

"I've known you for a long time, Ms. Sawyer," José surprised her by continuing to stand by her side. He furrowed his brows and looked Kirsten up and down. "I've seen you grow up. . . ."

"Yep!" Kirsten replied absentmindedly, still scanning the streets for a cab.

"And I have never seen you look so—" José

cut off as a cab pulled in front of the building. He opened the door and waited for Kirsten to climb inside.

"What?" Kirsten turned back to him before getting into the taxi. She was curious now. "What is it?"

"Well, I've never seen you look . . . so . . . lost," he admitted. "Are you sure you're okay?"

Kirsten nodded, but her heart sank. She felt like total crap at that moment. For some reason, her doorman's opinion shook her deeply. She slipped into the cab and mumbled WXRJ's address to her driver. As the cab sped away, Kirsten felt a pit in her stomach. The man who had been calling her cabs for the last seventeen years had summarized Kirsten Sawyer in one word: *lost*.

Kirsten pulled out a mirror from her purse and looked at her reflection: She looked awful. Her once sparkling brown eyes were now sunken and blank. Her shiny hair had lost its luster. Her skin was pale and pasty. She *did* look lost.

Kyle had invaded her dreams, her thoughts, and now, even her soul. Tears began

49

to stream down her face. *That's it. No more!* She pulled her cell phone out of her purse and quickly dialed a number.

"Precinct!" a shrill voice announced over the line.

"Detective Peterson, please," Kirsten pleaded between sobs. "I have new information on Paul Stone."

Kirsten sank into the backseat, wiped tears from her eyes, and tried to collect herself. It was the millionth time she'd called Detective Peterson, the young cop in charge of the Sam Byrne murder case, but this time Kirsten had something real.

"Homicide," Peterson rasped. His voice sounded tired, overworked.

"Hey. It's Kirsten," she said.

"How can I help you today, Ms. Sawyer?" Peterson asked.

Kirsten could hear someone was shouting in the precinct. She imagined Peterson standing next to the booking desk, taking time out of his crazy schedule to field yet *another* call from that psycho teenager.

Screw it, Kirsten told herself as she pressed on. *I've come this far. . . .*

"I think Kyle called me," she said.

"You think?" Peterson asked.

Kirsten wondered if he believed her at all. She looked outside the cab and shook her head. Her taxi was crawling through Midtown traffic. At this rate, running would get Kirsten to WXRJ faster.

"I imagine he didn't reveal any information about his *whereabouts* did he?" Peterson asked.

"No," Kirsten admitted.

"And did he threaten you in any way?"

"Not really, but—"

"Did he line up a place to meet with you, or another time he'd call?"

"No," Kirsten confessed. She was starting to feel stupid for calling. What new information did she really have, anyway?

"Listen, Ms. Sawyer," Peterson sighed. "I'll make a note of the phone call, and I *assure* you that my guys will continue to work on this. But until we have a more substantial lead, there's not much more I can do right now."

Kirsten stared at her face in the compact once more. She just wished it could all be over already. But unlike movies and dime-store thrillers, real life didn't wrap up conveniently. And, apparently, young detectives didn't always save the day. "Thanks, anyway," she said, but Peterson was already off the line.

Stuffing her cell phone back into her purse, Kirsten looked out of the greasy cab window. She was still five blocks away from work, and now they were stuck behind a garbage truck.

Kirsten gave the driver a twenty, opened the door, and ran the rest of the way to work. When she finally arrived at Studio Five, Kirsten was literally covered in sweat. And, much worse than that, Kate Grisholm was already in there, preparing to start the live show.

Kirsten ducked low behind the glass-paneled wall and sped through the hallway, barely evading her boss. Rounding the corner, she quietly slid into the tech studio and closed the door. *Close call,* she thought.

But then she heard him!

Brian. Even though it wasn't his job, he was setting up the phone log, checking Kate's computer. He was covering for Kirsten!

"Look what the cat dragged in," Brian kidded, looking up through his blond curls.

"Alarm clock didn't go off," Kirsten said, and immediately got to work. "Thanks for covering for me." She took over the task of getting the phone bank ready to start fielding calls.

"No problem," Brian winked as he moved out of her way and opened the door to leave.

Kirsten smiled at a curious Kate Grisholm out in the studio and gave her the thumbs-up signal.

"So, I'll see you—"

"Love Stinks," Kirsten interrupted Brian as she answered the first caller. She mouthed *sorry* to him as she typed the caller's name on her computer.

Checking to make sure Kate wasn't looking, Kirsten finally looked back at him. "I'm going to make this up to you," she whispered as the theme music to *Love Stinks* piped through the studio.

"I hope so," Brian said smiling.

Is he flirting? Kirsten wondered.

"There's a party this weekend out in the Hamptons. You should come," she said. "As my official invite. As a thank-you."

"Really?"

"Really," Kirsten said as she switched to the next call.

"That sounds cool," Brian said, smiling back. "Actually, I'm staying out there on the weekends, anyway. Over in Amagansett. Surfing."

"Well then, it's a date," Kirsten said.

"Is it?" Brian teased. He then moved to grab the envelope he'd left on the phone bank. He lingered as he reached right past Kirsten.

He smelled good. Really good.

Still close to her, Brian turned and whispered, "I like you, Kirsten."

"I thought you were an innocent Jersey Boy." Kirsten smiled.

"I *am* from Jersey, but I never said I was innocent." Brian winked again as he walked out of the tech room.

Wow. He really is cute, Kirsten thought with a slight grin as she sifted through a pile of prerecorded commercials. She liked Brian too. She liked him a lot. But was she ready for feelings like these?

The Zen fountain in Dr. Fitzgerald's office bubbled as usual. Kirsten found herself getting lost in its tranquil sound.

After a long, stressful day at WXRJ, Kirsten lay back on the sleek, black leather recliner and poured out her thoughts. "Brian's obviously sweet and nice and all that, but—"

"But *what?*" Dr. Fitzgerald smiled.

And Kirsten smiled too. She couldn't help it. Doctor Fitzgerald had found a way to win her confidence, and now Kirsten felt as if she were gossiping with a friend—to a point. She wasn't about to tell Fitzgerald about how she'd been partying nonstop for the past few weeks.

"I'm just not ready to get involved with another guy," Kirsten said. "Not yet."

"Fine. But I'm just saying you should keep your options open," Fitzgerald replied. "A little romance might be a nice distraction."

"With my luck, Brian will end up being a psychotic killer too!" Kirsten cracked.

"What if he's not?" Fitzgerald continued. "What if he's just a really good kisser?"

"Is this *The Bachelorette* or something?" Kirsten shot back. "Why are you so hot for me to start dating again?"

"It's not just about dating, Kirsten. It's about *living.* I'm just trying to get you to loosen up a little. Life won't move on until you *let it* move on."

"But how can I do that if I can't stop thinking about Sam?" Kirsten countered. Just mentioning her friend's name made her feel a lump in her throat.

"Have you visited Sam's parents since the murder?" Fitzgerald suddenly asked.

"No, not after the funeral," Kirsten admitted. "I haven't been able to bring myself to see them. I mean, come on. I lied about Sam staying over with me the night she was killed! Then I protected Kyle."

"You know, sometimes comforting someone else can be the best comfort for yourself," Dr. Fitzgerald said. "Maybe it's time you paid them a visit."

Maybe I should, Kirsten said to herself. It was a good idea—one that she hoped she had the courage to actually go through with. "All right." Kirsten looked at her watch. The hour was up. "If I'm going to move on, I'd better get a move on."

Dr. Fitzgerald tilted her head. "See you in a few days," she said.

Kirsten walked out of Dr. Fitzgerald's

office feeling lighter. Maybe relaxed for the first time in a while, even a little confident. She exited back onto Park Avenue and headed up Eighty-third Street, almost jogging with her newly found energy—until she slammed into someone.

"Whoa!" It was Scott, looking alarmed.

"Oops! Sorry!" Kirsten said. "What are you doing?"

Scott shrugged. "I'm just doing a little favor for my kid sister. How about you?"

Kirsten frowned. She didn't want to tell Scott that she was seeing a psychiatrist, even though she knew he'd be cool about it.

"Hey. You all right, Kirsten?" Scott asked. "Did Kyle call you again or something?"

"No, no . . . nothing like that," Kirsten said. "Let's change the subject. What's up at the Party Room?"

Scott broke into a grin. "Well, we're having a tiki theme tonight. It's a little weird, I know, but I'm making awesome piña coladas. The manager is actually buying *real* coconuts this time!"

Kirsten recalled what Scott's mojitos had done to her the other night. "Sounds like fun."

"So will I see you there, or what?" Scott asked, playfully punching her in the arm.

He didn't have to ask twice.

"Beam me up, Scotty!" Kirsten smiled. "I'm there!"

8

Later that night Kirsten

lit a joint that Leslie had given her and inhaled deeply as she listened to the rain hit the roof of her penthouse apartment. Her parents had long since gone to sleep, and she needed something to take the edge off. She was sick of Dr. Fitzgerald's sleeping pills, and after a crazy night of partying, she needed something to help her relax. She exhaled the smoke into a sheet of Downy fabric softener to mask the scent. An old boarding school trick Julie's older brother, Chad, had taught them before heading off to military school.

Kirsten relaxed into the thick down covers of her bed, letting the air-conditioning blast her into oblivion, and rehashed another night at the Party Room. She could still see herself and Julie learning how to hula dance, surrounded by a pack of salivating guys and laughing between sips of Scott's fresh piña coladas. Kirsten also remembered Brandon Yardley wearing a stupid yellow lei and trying to corner her all night.

Thank God *he left early,* she thought as the pot started taking effect. Her eyelids became heavier as she listened to a distant siren out on the street. *Chill,* she kept telling herself. *It's time for some* real *sleep.*

Kirsten finished the joint, smudged it out in a Diet Coke can, and waved smoke out of the air. She rolled out of bed and took off her slinky red Marc Jacobs dress. *I looked good tonight,* she thought as she let the raw silk curl to the floor. She yawned and opened the door to her walk-in closet.

She stepped inside and reached to flick on the light, but it was already on. *Weird,* she thought. *I never leave the light on in my closet.*

Then Kirsten heard a hanger drop near the back of the closet. Out of the corner of her eye she saw some clothes move! She gasped and backed up in a frenzy of motion. Clothes seemed to grab at her as she fought her way out of the closet.

As fear ripped through her, Kirsten ran out

of her room. The hallway lights were off, but she didn't stop for a second. "Aghh!"

"What's going on?" Gil Sawyer grumbled, coming out of the master bedroom. Daddy wasn't exactly the nurturing type. He smelled of pipe smoke and NyQuil. Kirsten's most consistent childhood memory of her father was sitting outside his study, waiting for *permission* to give him her latest scribbled artwork.

"In my room!" Kirsten screamed at her father.

Kirsten's mother, Susan, rushed out of the bedroom. "What's wrong, Kirsten?" she cried.

"Someone's in my room!" Kirsten shivered.

"Oh, my God!" Mrs. Sawyer grabbed her daughter and held her as tightly as possible.

"You sure?" Mr. Sawyer asked.

"Go check, Gil!" Mrs. Sawyer snapped, shoving her husband forward.

Mr. Sawyer sighed in annoyance and marched toward Kirsten's room. He never believed Kirsten, and nothing could get his heart rate above two beats per minute, anyway.

"Careful, Dad!" Kirsten held her breath as her father walked down the long hallway and disappeared into her bedroom.

"Dad?" she called out after a few minutes of silence. After a few seconds of Kirsten imagining the absolute worst, however, her father shuffled back out of Kirsten's room.

"Couldn't find a thing," he said with a frown.

Kirsten felt her body go weak as her father shuffled past her, back to sleep. *I really* am *going nuts,* she thought. Well, she was also stoned, so maybe it was just paranoia.

"I know what you need, sweetie," Mrs. Sawyer said. She took her daughter's hand and led her into the kitchen. She sat Kirsten down on a stool and hummed softly as she boiled a pot of water.

"You've been going to all of your therapy sessions, right?" her mom quietly inquired. She sounded like she was talking to a scared fifth grader.

"Yes," Kirsten said, feeling totally pathetic since it was clear that her mom *and* her dad thought she was nuts too.

"Here. This will calm you down," Kirsten's mother said warmly as she handed Kirsten a cup of cocoa.

Cocoa. Mom's cure for everything.

"Thanks. This will definitely help." Kirsten played along and took a small sip from the cup. Maybe this made her mother feel better, but Kirsten knew what *she* needed to really calm down.

"How about some nice graham crackers?" her mom asked. When she walked into the pantry for a moment, Kirsten rushed into the library—to the liquor cabinet—and poured a generous helping of Ketel One into her drink and headed back to her bedroom.

She couldn't deal anymore. How could she? She was seventeen years old and she had already lost her mind. Maybe she should just buy the straitjacket now and be done with it. She bet she could get something in a nice shade of purple from Prada's fall collection.

Kirsten drowsily entered her bedroom. She shut off the light and collapsed on her bed and sighed. Just before drifting off to sleep, she rolled over and noticed that her closet door was still open and the light was still on.

Kirsten huffed as she stumbled to her feet. She walked into the closet and reached for the string that led to the overhead light. As she stretched to pull the cord, she lost her balance and fell into her winter clothing rack.

Whoa—spins, Kirsten thought, sliding down the wall of the closet to the floor. She leaned over and rested her head on the plush mauve rug. *Better . . . much better.*

And then she saw it—right in the center of the carpet.

A fresh muddy footprint.

Someone *had* been there!

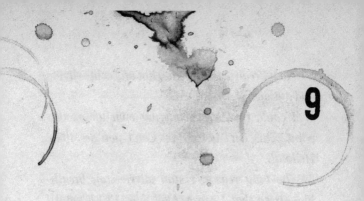

9

That's right!

Be afraid. Be very afraid.

I don't care if that's a cliché.

I don't care about a goddamn thing right now, as a matter of fact.

All I care about is keeping control. Keeping my head on straight. Keeping my plan in sight.

I've got you right where I want you!

Are you FREAKING BLIND?

God, I could use a drink. But I won't. I won't weaken myself like you do. I'll keep strong. And wait. For the perfect chance.

Perfect.

Yeah, right!

I remember I used to believe in perfect. A happy family. Christmas glee—the whole phony package. I used to actually believe that there was right and wrong out there in the world.

Now I realize there's only hot and cold—living and dying.

I could care less about my own life at this point. This isn't about me! Can't you see that? Hello!!!!!

The only reason I stay alive—stay breathing—is so that I can MAKE YOU FEEL what I feel every day.

Why am I even wasting my breath on you?

Like you give a shit.

You probably think I'm the villain. You probably still believe in heroes just like everyone else.

Well, here's a news flash: Batman and Robin were into S&M. Superman was a perv in a costume, flying around looking for hot chicks to nail.

Heroes are dead.

And so . . . are . . . you.

I'm still cold. Still in control. Calm, even. Ahhhh . . .

Sure, we might've had a close call or two, and sure, my hands might be shaking all over this goddamn page, but trust me:

It's because I'm excited. Exhilarated!

The end of this story is already written.

And I have the pen. . . .

10

"Way to go, Sawyer!" Julie cheered as she moshed to a White Stripes song blasting through the Hamptons party. "Go for it! Brian's a total hottie!"

"Chill, Julie!" Kirsten blushed. "I'm not ready yet."

The two girls stood in the center of Clark Gansevoort's summer rager—the house party to end all house parties that his parents let him throw every year despite the thousands of dollars it cost them in puke stains alone.

"Not ready?" Julie teased. "What're you talking about, slut? You're the one who invited him!"

"I just need some time," Kirsten whined, pushing Julie away. She knew why Julie was so juiced up in the first place: She had a plan to hook up with Clark at least once this summer. Her beefcake crush had just graduated from

Talcott and was headed for Harvard on a football scholarship.

As Julie continued to dance circles around her, Kirsten watched Brian from across the crowded room, nursing a beer and nodding his head to the music. He didn't quite fit with the Richie Rich kids who made out on antique wicker furniture, did keg stands in the vast *Architectural Digest*–like kitchen, snorted coke in the master bedroom, and tried on Mrs. Gansevoort's tacky golf outfits. And he didn't seem to know anyone—except Kirsten, who at this point in time was kind of feeling like a freak and wondering why the hell she'd invited him there, anyway.

"Come on, girl!" Julie pressed on. "You need a *healthy distraction*! Isn't that what your shrink keeps saying?"

"You mean my *psychiatrist*?" Kirsten corrected Julie. Her best friend was cruising for a serious bruising tonight.

"You say tomato, I say to-maaaahh-to," Julie sang.

"Ugh," was all Kirsten could get out as she slammed a glass of wine.

Too embarrassed for words, Kirsten stalked off into another room, avoiding Brian altogether. *Smooth move*, she chided herself as she searched out the bar.

And no surprise whatsoever, Leslie Fenk was already there. She was dressed to kill— Versace everything—flirting with Clark's two older brothers. Kirsten remembered them from last year's bash. They were both Harvard boys, too, and their names were Chauncey and Reginald, or Mortimer and Tanner or something equally WASPy.

Kirsten snuck up behind Leslie and slipped her hands over her eyes.

"I smell Dior," Leslie said, playing detective. She reached up to touch Kirsten's hands. "That could only mean one thing," she hummed. "It's a Woodley girl!" Leslie spun around and gave Kirsten a big hug and a kiss, lingering a few seconds with her arms around her waist.

Slow down, Fenk, Kirsten thought as Clark's brothers drooled. She backed off a little. She remembered the last time that she went out with Leslie. Pretending to hook up to avoid Brandon Yardley was one thing, but being

Leslie's latest plaything was altogether something else.

The brothers Gansevoort high-fived and left Kirsten and Leslie alone.

"Glad to see you," Leslie purred. She reached into her handbag and found two tiny tabs of Ecstasy. "Take both at once and call me in the morning," Leslie joked.

"Now we're talking!" Kirsten cheered.

Kirsten had taken E only once before—with Sam. She knew exactly what it did: It made you all hot and tingly—every sensation was bigger and better. Kirsten winked at Leslie, placing both pills on her tongue.

An hour and a bottle of Cristal later, and Kirsten stumbled outside to the pool area. As she watched a splashing and shouting chicken fight in Clark's Olympic-size pool, she laughed out loud. Her head swam with a warm liquid sensation, and a giddy shiver crawled across her chest.

God, I feel gooood! Kirsten thought as she looked around for Brian. *Time to find my crush.* She giggled. She spotted Brian dancing next to the pool. An Outkast song blared from a set of enormous loudspeakers.

Kirsten could literally *feel* the beat on her skin.

Brian looked much more comfortable now that he was dancing to a hip-hop track. In fact, he had great rhythm. Kirsten licked her lips. A huge grin spread across her face as she approached him.

At first, Brian didn't see Kirsten walking along the side of the pool. He was busy dancing with two Chapin Prep girls, keeping both of them plenty interested while also keeping a respectful distance. Kirsten wondered if Brian was too good to be true.

"Brian!" Kirsten yelled out, swelling with courage. She made her way to him, gently edging the Chapin sluts out of the way, and started dancing with Brian.

Closer and closer.

Kirsten felt the music grow louder. She felt amazing. When Brian grabbed her hands and started swaying with her, Kirsten felt a wave of tingles run up her arms.

The bass line seemed to appear in front of her eyes, rattling the world in a melodic, magical way. As the deejay mixed in another song, something Kirsten didn't recognize, Brian grabbed her by the waist.

Hello.

They dipped to the music, moving in lazy, hip synchronicity. Kirsten knew they looked good together. Taking things to the next level, she ran her hand up the back of Brian's neck, grabbing at his blond curls. He didn't seem to mind at all.

Then Kirsten stepped back so that Brian could watch her moves. She raised her arms above her head, swaying her hips and moving in sync with he beat. She spun around and—

"W-w-w-whoa!" Kirsten's arms flailed in the air as she lost her balance and teetered by the edge of the pool. She reached out for Brian's hand but before he could snatch her up, she crashed backward into the water with a big splash.

As Kirsten surfaced in her now-ruined dress and gasped for breath, everyone broke into laughter. She slammed her fist into the water and glanced back at Brian, totally humiliated.

He reached out his hand to help her, but he was laughing right along with the others.

"Screw you guys!" Kirsten cried. She wasn't really mad at Brian or the partygoers.

As the warm fuzzy feeling from the Ecstasy gave way to a burning sensation of embarrassment, she waded out of the pool and rushed back inside the house.

"Hey, Kirsten! Wait up!" Brian called to her, but she ignored his shouts and scanned the house for Julie.

Time to GO! Kirsten felt trapped under her skin. Everyone seemed to be staring at her, but she didn't stop racing from kitchen to living room to master bedroom to home theater. *Where the hell are you, Jules?*

Kirsten almost ran into Brian as she approached the basement door.

"Kirsten! Are you okay?" he asked, trying to slow her down.

"Not okay," Kirsten said, pushing her date out of the way. She opened the door to the "off-limits" basement and ran down the steps. She lost her footing halfway down, slipped, and slid down the rest of the way. "Shit!"

Eight ball, corner pocket.

Or was that right leg, side pocket?

On top of the Gansevoorts' antique pool table, Julie lay underneath Clark's linebacker body, making out and feeling him up without a care in the world.

Kirsten glanced around the room: Neon beer signs flickered in the corners. Budweiser Girls winked at the NASCAR drivers posing on the opposite wall.

Pulling herself up and massaging her bruised ass, Kirsten coughed, clapped, stomped, and snapped for two full minutes, but Julie and Clark weren't about to be interrupted. Finally Kirsten screamed, "I've got to get out of here, Julie!" and her friend looked up.

Julie's face was a smear of makeup, and Clark cursed to himself as he stared daggers at Kirsten. Julie winked at Kirsten and mouthed *please?* as Clark began kissing her neck again.

However bad her friend's taste was, Kirsten knew that Julie wasn't going anywhere— probably for the whole night.

Ugghh! Kirsten could have screamed, but instead, she bit her tongue. She knew that her friend had wanted to get with Clark for a long time. Simply put, Julie Pembroke was a selfish bitch when she was "getting some."

Kirsten gave up and hurried back up the

staircase. Her dress was cold and wet and it stuck to her legs as she ran.

Once again, Kirsten rushed by Brian, unable to deal with her growing embarrassment. To make it worse, she was starting to feel a little woozy. And Kirsten *did not* want to be known as the girl who fell in the pool, then puked after she saw Julie and Clark practically *doing it* in the basement. Out of options, frustrated and angry, Kirsten booked through the marble foyer and burst outside the front door.

As tears welled in her eyes, Kirsten stood on the expansive Gansevoort lawn and remembered something. She reached into her sopping-wet Gucci purse and fished out Julie's car keys. Julie didn't have any pockets, so she'd asked Kirsten to hold them.

Stumbling toward Julie's parents' new Porsche Cayenne, Kirsten fumbled with the alarm until the SUV beeped open. Just as Kirsten reached the vehicle and climbed-fell inside, a deafening bolt of thunder rippled through the sky.

In the rush to get inside, 'cause she wasn't wet enough already, Kirsten dropped the keys under the front seat. "Stupid!"

After spending the next few seconds scrambling for the keys, Kirsten started up the Porsche. It roared to life as rain started hammering against the windshield.

Even with a storm falling all around her, Kirsten couldn't think about anything except that look on Brian's face as he'd laughed at her. "I'm pathetic!" she said as she jammed the SUV into reverse and skidded across the driveway.

Barely missing a wrought-iron statue standing guard at the entrance to the Gansevoorts' driveway, Kirsten gained control of the Cayenne just in time to swerve onto the main road, demolishing the corner of Clark's large front hedge.

Just get away, her mind spun. *Get home.* The tears came faster now. *I made a total ass of myself. I'm a total screwup!* She swerved as she wiped snot from under her nose. She was sobbing now. *A wreck. A total wreck . . .*

Kirsten slammed on the gas and took off faster into the stormy night. *Forget Brian! Forget ever dating at all!* Lost in her head, she ignored the angry honk of a driver whizzing by her in the opposite lane. Her tears started to flood her eyes, making it harder to see.

Rain. Lightning. Wind.

The storm was now right on top of her. Kirsten swerved again as a strong gust brought a sheet of rain across her window.

Feeling the tug of fear, Kirsten downshifted the Porsche. The gears whined as the SUV jerked into a slower pace. *I don't want to die tonight,* she thought.

But just as Kirsten started to travel at a more reasonable pace, another lighting bolt crackled right in front of her.

Kirsten screamed out and swerved again. This time she struggled to gain control of the vehicle. Her sight returned to her—just in time to see a U-Haul truck coming right at her.

"Noooo!" Kirsten yanked the steering wheel to the side as the truck squeezed by her left, barely missing the driver's side mirror.

Behind her now, the U-Haul swerved safely back off the shoulder of the road where Kirsten had carelessly forced him. Adjusting her rearview mirror, Kirsten breathed a sigh of relief, shook her head, and watched the truck disappear around a curve in the road.

Then she turned her attention back to the road ahead.

"Oh, my God!" she yelled. Something was standing right on the yellow stripes, not five yards in front of her! Kirsten slammed on the brakes with every living ounce of energy she had.

SCREEECH!

11

A deer stared peacefully
at Kirsten through the rain-splattered windshield. After a few moments, a knobby-kneed
fawn caught up to its mother, and the two ani-
mals bounded off the road.

I could've killed someone. . . . Kirsten's stomach churned at the realization. *I could've killed
myself!*

Fully stopped now, Kirsten turned off the
Porsche and buried her head in her hands.
She started to sob. Hard. Harder than she had
in months. Kirsten's ribs hurt as she gasped
for air.

After a long while, Kirsten started the SUV
again and pulled it to the side of the road. She
was way too messed up to drive. Getting
behind the wheel in her state was quite possibly the stupidest choice she had ever made.

Just as Kirsten pushed her seat back and

prepared to pass out right there on the side of the pitch-black roadway—a bright light illuminated the inside of the Porsche. She quickly ducked down in her seat. *What if it's the cops?* The last thing she needed was a DWI.

When Kirsten heard brakes slamming on behind her, however, she shot up in her seat. *Now what?* she wondered.

A dark figure ran toward the Cayenne through the heavy rain.

Kirsten ducked again, hoping whoever it was might think the car was empty. When the mystery person tapped lightly on the window, waited, and tapped again, however, Kirsten slowly found the courage to sit up and look through the tinted glass.

"Need a lift?" Brian asked, smiling.

Kirsten let out a breath. *Thank God it's Brian,* she thought. *Wait a sec, wasn't he the one I was trying to get away from in the first place? Oh, yeah. He was.*

Her face instantly began to flush as the whole embarrassing scene at the party flashed in her brain.

"I saw you leave the party. Are you okay?" Brian added as Kirsten rolled down the window.

"I'm just resting," Kirsten said. *God, that was lame,* she thought.

"Let me drive you home," Brian insisted.

However embarrassed Kirsten might've been, she wasn't about to get behind the wheel again that night. And Brian insisted on driving the Porsche to Julie's beach house and walking the two or so miles back to get his car.

When Brian pulled into the Pembrokes' driveway, he hopped out of the Porsche and opened Kirsten's door for her. He escorted her up the cobblestone pathway right up to the wide farmhouse entrance, then they both stopped outside.

Kirsten felt her face turn red again. The tingle of Ecstasy was still working through her bloodstream. She knew she looked horrible, and she felt even worse now.

He must think I'm a total loser, Kirsten thought as Brian stared into her eyes.

"You can dance, girl," Brian said, surprising her. Then he made some kind of surfer signal with his hand.

"What are you doing?" Kirsten laughed.

"Hang loose, yo!" Brian flashed her the sign again.

Kirsten did her best to imitate the gesture, but her version came out looking more like a broken garden trowel.

Brian laughed, took Kirsten's hand, and showed her how to make the sign. "Like this," he whispered, close to her ear.

"Oh," was all Kirsten could say, his voice sending delicious shivers from her ears all the way down to her toes. But then Kirsten remembered the pool again. "Listen, Brian. I want to apologize. I got way too messed up tonight, and—"

"Stop, Kirsten," Brian gently interrupted her. "You don't have to say anything."

"Yeah right," Kirsten exhaled, moving away from Brian. "I thought I could handle myself, and instead I—"

"Went pool hopping!" Brian smiled again. "It's cool, Kirsten. I only laughed because it was a funny moment. I wasn't laughing at *you.*"

"Really?" Kirsten asked, still feeling a little less defeated. "I'm glad, because—"

Then Brian leaned in and kissed her. A tender and passionate kiss. Kirsten enjoyed his soft lips for a moment, but then slowly pulled away.

"Oh . . . sorry." Brian frowned. It was his turn to flush with embarrassment. "I thought . . ."

Kirsten's mind scrambled to find the right words. "No. It's not you, Brian. Really," she assured him. "I just can't . . . *do this* right now." She really liked this guy, but she had too much other stuff that needed to be sorted out before she could be with anyone. She wasn't ready. She knew that now. "I need to clear my head first. Right now I'm just too confused."

Brian's face sank.

So did Kirsten's. She didn't want Brian to take it the wrong way, but it would be impossible to explain the whole situation. "It's not like I don't *want* to . . . I just—"

"It's cool," Brian said. Rubbing the back of his neck, he turned to leave.

Kirsten didn't want to see him go, but what could she do? "I'm not trying to mess with your head or anything!" she called out.

Brian turned back to face her one last time. "See you at work," he said flatly, and was gone.

Kirsten shook her head and slowly opened the front door to Julie's place. Things hadn't worked out the way she had planned. But then again, what *was* working out these days? Once inside, Kirsten shut the door and leaned against it. She rubbed her temples and let out a long sigh.

I'm lucky to be alive, she thought as she locked the door. Images of passing cars and skidding tires flashed through her mind. She tossed Julie's keys onto a couch in her living room and crossed into the kitchen. Turning on the overhead light, she pulled a teakettle from a top shelf and filled it with water.

Kirsten thought of her mother's cocoa. She hadn't even tasted it before spiking it with vodka. She set the kettle on the stove and then searched through the cupboards above the sink for tea. Nothing.

Kirsten then turned and walked over to the Pembrokes' English pantry.

She pushed the swinging door open and let out a piercing scream.

Kyle! He stood just two feet away from her, waiting in the dark.

12

Kirsten screamed again

as Kyle advanced toward her. His eyes looked wild and desperate. His wavy brown hair was drenched from the storm.

I'm trapped! Kirsten's mind screamed.

She bolted out of the pantry and slammed right into the stove. The teakettle toppled off its burner, splashing steaming water all over the floor, spattering Kirsten's legs with pain. "Get away from me!" she cried, running into the living room. "I'll call the police!"

Kyle followed, not saying a word and staring at her with hard and angry eyes.

Kirsten raced to the door and fumbled with the locks. *Have to get out of here!*

"Who was that guy?" Kyle finally spat out. He was angry. Very angry. He must have been lurking outside when Kirsten returned home with Brian.

Kirsten turned and faced him, her back against the door, "N-n-no one!" she stammered.

"Was that your boyfriend?" Kyle demanded.

"No, it wasn't. Please, Kyle!" Kirsten was crying now—couldn't hold it back any longer. She was all alone in a house with a killer. The wind was whipping outside. For a moment, Kirsten thought of Brian, but he was long gone by now.

Then she reached for the doorknob and twisted it and yanked open the door. *Run!* she thought. *Run, Kirsten, run!*

But before she could get five steps, Kyle grabbed her and squeezed her tight in his strong arms. Desperate, Kirsten bit Kyle on the arm and tried to knee him in the groin. Kyle screamed out in pain, but he was simply too powerful.

He dragged her, kicking and screaming, back into the farmhouse, slammed the front door shut, and locked it. Then he turned around and faced her.

Flooded with panic, Kirsten fell back against the couch and tensed her whole body. She closed her eyes. *It's going to happen. He's going to kill me right now!*

But then there was a pause.

A long pause.

Kirsten could hear Kyle breathing. He was just waiting for something.

For what? Kirsten thought as she slowly opened her eyes.

Kyle was now sitting on the floor, exhaling deeply. He wrung his hands and looked at her, clearly trying to figure out what to say.

Kirsten jumped up and made a run for the back door. She was fully crying now, screaming, "No! No! No!" over and over again.

Kyle leaped up from the floor and gave chase. He caught up to her in the kitchen and didn't let her go this time. "I'm not going to hurt you!"

The wind rushed out of Kirsten's lungs. She felt beaten, broken.

"Just listen!" Kyle pleaded in desperation. "Please."

"Why should I?" Kirsten shouted back.

"Because I'm innocent!"

"Bullshit!" Kirsten cried, sobbing harder now. "You've lied to me from the start."

Kyle held on as she kicked, clawed, and pushed her way around the kitchen. "Just . . .

just don't . . . be afraid," he said. "I just came here to tell you the truth."

"No . . . ," Kirsten repeated herself, weakening in Kyle's arms. She slowly stopped struggling. "I can't . . ."

"If you still don't believe me after what I tell you, then you can turn me in, okay?" Kyle added with a tired voice. "I won't fight it."

Alone in the middle of nowhere, surrounded by howling winds and empty roads, Kirsten knew that there was nowhere to go. Kyle must've been following her for days, waiting for the perfect moment to show up. She remembered the footprint in her closet. God only knew how he got into her white-glove building, much less her penthouse apartment.

But now that he was here, she saw something . . . tender in his eyes. He looked fragile and vulnerable.

There was nothing else to do but listen, Kirsten decided. She would hear Kyle's story and hope that he remained calm. At this point, the best and only path was the one of least resistance.

Kirsten pulled back from Kyle's grasp and leaned against the kitchen counter. Avoiding eye contact, Kirsten crossed her arms and waited for an explanation. "Okay, Kyle," she finally said. "What?"

Kyle sat against the kitchen table, brushed the overgrown bangs out of his eyes, and began: "The truth isn't pretty, but it's *true*." He cleared his throat before continuing. "I was in love with this girl, Carolee. I'll never forget her. . . ." Kyle swallowed, clearly affected. "Carolee Adams was my first love, my high school sweetheart."

Kirsten softened her stance and started to listen. Something about the calm, honest tone in Kyle's voice was setting her at ease.

"I saw her at the first dance of sophomore year. Carolee was this amazing, cool, smart freshman, and as soon as I met her, I knew she'd be my girlfriend."

Kirsten caught herself smiling slightly. Kyle was a romantic at heart.

Kyle then sat down in a chair next to the table. He took off his drenched flannel shirt; an undershirt clung to his muscular frame. "Now it's my senior year, okay? I'm an all-state point guard on the basketball team with a 3.7 GPA. I'm a lock for a full ride at Brown.

89

I've been dating Carolee for three years and I am practically married to her by now. Life is cool. Better than cool. Honestly, I thought I was living the high school fantasy . . . until one night . . . the night that changed my life forever. . . ."

As Kyle told her his story, Kirsten could picture the night in question three years ago—back when Kyle was Paul Stone . . . a senior banquet . . . a beautiful spring night . . . hanging out with close friends . . .

How could things have gone so wrong . . . ?

Part Two

13

Kyle is Paul . . .

Paul Stone.

And Paul Stone is walking across Seventy-ninth Street, heading to the Zoo with his boys.

Not a kid's zoo. *The* Zoo: the tightest hip-hop club on the Upper East Side.

It's Friday night, right after Talcott Preparatory School's Senior Banquet. It's the last weekend before graduation, and therefore, the last weekend to *rage*.

As he and The Crew—Moyer, Goldstein, Willett, and Schloss—hurry down Lex, sharing not-so-furtive swigs from a bottle of Captain Morgan, Paul laughs as his friends rip on one another's mothers:

"The bitch is *so* fat." Willett jams a finger into Schloss's back. "She jumped up in the air and got stuck!"

Everyone laughs, giving Willett pounds.

"Oh, yeah?" Schloss says. "Well . . . your mom is dumb!" Schloss has *no* skills playing the game.

"Schloss," Paul teases, "is that the best you can come up with?"

"That's what your mom said last night!" Schloss counters, shoving his friends as he laughs.

In the middle of chugging rum, Paul breaks into laughter, spraying the sticky liquor all over himself. "Wait. What the hell does that even *mean*?" he asks, scrunching up his face. "You're saying that my mom took one look at your shriveled-ass thing and kicked you out of bed?"

"Damn, Paul!" Moyer sucks his teeth. "Quit overanalyzing the mother jokes!"

"Yeah, bro!" echoes Goldstein. He always copies Moyer. "You're not in AP English right now, bitch!"

The guys always bust Paul about being a nerd. But though he knows he's different from the last-name-only guys he rolls with, Paul Stone is loyal to the core. Ever since making varsity as a sophomore, Paul's been inseparable from his b-ball crew.

Paul smiles as they walk down the street. It's a big day of celebration. Four years of Talcott and soon he'll be free.

The only thing I'll really miss at that place is Carolee, he thinks. Paul can't wait to see her at the party. They've been planning this night forever. He thinks about dancing with her, holding her, kissing her and, eventually, taking her home.

Even though Paul's going to be in Rhode Island next year, he plans on driving back every weekend. He'll make the relationship work no matter what.

Finally, The Crew arrives at the Zoo. As expected, a huge line snakes out of the entrance. Every single high school girl in America waits outside, dressed in hip huggers, Tommy Girl skirts, and far too much makeup. But lucky for Paul, Moyer knows the door guy. Without so much as a moment's hesitation, he and the others slip inside.

On the other side of the velvet curtains, Paul enters a dark, black-lit club thick with smoke and overdone bass. As Jay-Z vibrates, he weaves his way through a wall of wannabe thugs near the entrance.

Although someone leans into his shoulder, trying to start something, Paul simply bounces off and keeps on walking. He could care less about fighting tonight. *Tonight is all about Carolee.*

Paul makes his way into the heart of the club and looks around. The place is packed with Talcott seniors. Everyone is tossing back drinks, screaming out, "Seniors rule!" and dancing with reckless abandon. They're letting out the stress they've accumulated over four years of essays, late-night studying, and five thousand extracurriculars.

"Pretty hot, huh?" Willett bumps into Paul with shots of Patrón.

"Hell, yeah!" Paul agrees as he slams the drink with his friend. He rocks backward and then slings an arm around his friend. Paul's happy to be out. Happy to be celebrating. Happy to be alive.

The only thing missing is his girlfriend.

Where is she? Paul wonders. He's starting to get nervous. He always feels better with Carolee by his side. She takes care of him. She makes him feel loved, special—all that greeting-card stuff. For Paul, a relationship is more than just sex. "Where is she?" Paul finally shouts.

"Who?" Willett asks through a long burp.

"Carolee!" Who else would he be looking for? "She was supposed to meet me near the entrance."

"Right over there." Moyer moshes into his two friends, then stretches out an arm and points across the dance floor.

At first, Paul can't track where Moyer is pointing. It's too dark to see. A strobe light blurs his vision.

When the lights flash bright red, however, Paul sees her. Carolee's right in the middle of the dance floor, wearing a backless nothing, grinding with some guy!

What the hell?

And then it gets worse! Seemingly having the time of her life, Carolee laughs and whispers into the guy's ear. And the guy grabs Carolee around the waist!

As his friends start to laugh, Paul's face contorts. *It's our night!* his mind screams. A searing streak of anger runs through Paul as he rushes into the mob of partiers.

"Watch it, dude!" someone yells as he plows

97

through, stumbling from his last tequila.

Without thinking, Paul yanks the pair apart, grabbing Carolee forcefully by the arm. "What do you think you're doing, Carolee?" he screams, attracting everyone's attention.

Carolee's face flushes red as she spins away from Paul.

From anger? Guilt? What?

"Stop it, Paul!" she shouts.

"What the hell are you *doing*?" Paul reaches for her again, mad-dogging the guy she's been dancing with.

"Just calm down!" Carolee yells back, clearly tipsy. She looks as beautiful as ever: milky skin, blond hair, green eyes. But now, Carolee's beauty infuriates Paul.

As much as Paul loves his girlfriend, he hates her in that moment.

"Who the hell are *you*?" Paul shouts at the guy as he rolls up his sleeves, ready to go right then and there.

Before the guy can defend himself, Carolee jumps between the two boys. "Steve's just a friend!" she stammers, pushing against Paul's chest.

Something about Toronto, something about camp and "catching up," but Paul's barely listening. He's too busy grilling Carolee suspiciously. "Why didn't you tell me you had a visitor?" Paul pushes.

"I don't know!" Carolee cries out. "Just chill, okay? I guess it slipped my mind or something! Is that a crime?"

Why is she being so defensive?

"You want to see a crime?" Paul yells as he shoves Steve. He imagines Steve's skull splitting on the sidewalk outside. Blood covering his new Jordans. An ambulance.

Steve careens into a group of girls, falling to the floor. He looks pathetic, and—*damn it*—innocent!

What's happening to me? Paul thinks. He never loses control like this.

Finally Steve gets up: "Hey, buddy. Sorry about this. We're just camp friends."

And to Paul's burning embarrassment, Steve has a thick Canadian accent. "Steve," he adds, extending his hand for an international treaty.

Why's he have to be so goddamn nice? Paul thinks. He feels like a total asshole now.

Carolee stares daggers at Paul. She's been moody lately, but Paul always assumed it was because he was leaving for Brown soon.

"Welcome to America," Paul mutters as he walks off angrily to the bar. His neck feels hot with embarrassment. But even if Carolee and Steve are just friends, what's with this dirty dancing?

Got to get a drink, Paul thinks. Even though he usually knows his limits, tonight he's going to drink right past them.

At the bar, Moyer stops harassing yet another girl for a moment and turns to his friend. "You're gonna let Carolee play you like that?" Moyer shouts, already on his second shot of Jägermeister. "She's too hot to trust, son!"

Paul takes off his Talcott tie and tosses it onto the bar. He slams a shot of Jäger, but then turns back toward Moyer. "Wait. What'd you just say?" Paul asks.

Moyer isn't paying attention, now. He's too busy staring at Carolee on the dance floor.

"Oh! I get it!" Paul pushes Moyer. "You're into her, too, aren't you?"

"What?" Moyer laughs it off. "Bros before hoes, man!"

Am I going crazy? Paul asks himself. He's overreacting again. "Sorry," he finally says, and tries to calm down. *Carolee's just upset about my leaving. She still loves me. She's . . .* Paul's thoughts trails off as he looks back across the dance floor. *Carolee? Where's Carolee!*

She's not on the dance floor anymore. And neither is Steve!

Leaving Moyer at the bar, Paul hurries through the club. He scans everywhere, but doesn't find them. Then Paul remembers the downstairs section of the Zoo—the almost-pitch-black basement where he and Carolee sneaked off the last time they were there.

Paul finds the back stairwell and hurries down into the dark storage area. He stumbles through stacks of champagne crates and empty kegs, seething with anger.

How could Carolee play me like this? Paul thinks. *On my biggest night of the year!*

In the distance, there's a soft light glowing from behind a large, opaque glass door. Paul hurries forward and pulls on the handle. It's locked.

Just as Paul turns to leave, he hears a giggle on the other side of the door.

Carolee!

Paul yanks on the door again, but it doesn't budge.

More giggling.

Paul loses it. He jams the butt of his hand directly through the glass!

Shards spray everywhere. Blood spiders across Paul's fist as he steps through the doorway, searching for a light. He throws on a switch to find Carolee, *his* girlfriend, hooking up with Steve!

They're sprawled across a table, pawing each other in a large, empty room.

Paul can't believe his eyes. *How could I be such an idiot?* he thinks, running his bloody hand through his hair.

Carolee and Steve just freeze, like two rats caught raiding the trash.

Trash! Paul bounds toward them.

Steve, slight but sober, dodges Paul's first charge and sends him flying into a stack of chairs.

"Paul!" Carolee screams as her boyfriend makes a second lunge at Steve.

They start to wrestle, cracking through the Sheetrock walls as they whirl about.

After a few moments of intense struggle and Carolee's constant screaming, people start running into the room from upstairs.

Way past anger, Paul spits blood and tackles Steve into a stand of bar stools. Yanking his hair, Paul lands a few solid punches. His blood mixes with Steve's, a coldhearted crowd cheering them on now.

Finally, two hefty bouncers dive through the crowd. Paul breaks away, but the bouncers grab him, anyway. D-Train, the larger of the two giants, gets in a few stomach shots on Paul.

Ooof! Paul sinks to his knees.

Suddenly Carolee lunges toward Paul and slaps him hard across the face. "We're over!" she screams, and then turns to comfort Steve.

Paul tries to make a run for Carolee, but D-Train puts him in a sleeper hold and pushes him to the floor. Then Carolee pulls Steve by the arm and rushes out.

As Paul watches Carolee escape, fixing her

slutty shirt, he slams his hand against the concrete floor. "I'll kill you, Carolee!" he screams in front of some fifty witnesses.

And the bouncers put the final hurt on him.

14

Hammered. Really hammered.

The tacky red chili lights in Tropixxx, a seedy bridge-and-tunnel bar down on Fifty-ninth Street and Second Avenue blur above Paul Stone. He tries to focus on one strand, tries to regain his clarity, but everything's on spin-cycle.

The whole useless world is in constant motion.

It's over, Paul keeps chanting to himself over and over again, keeping upright by holding on to Moyer's shoulder. "I should've strangled that punk!" he says through his teeth.

"Yeah, you should have!" Moyer adds. "But at least you got in some good shots, bro."

"Who even cares?" Paul says. "It's over!" Pain swells in his neck and back and ribs, but that doesn't stop him from slamming another shot of Jäger. He barely feels the burning liquid go down.

It's over, Paul thinks again as he envisions Carolee's last horrible expression before she dumped him. *How long has she been cheating on me?* he wonders.

Next to the bar, the rest of The Crew has cornered a young public school girl on the dance floor. Gina *something* dances carefree with the pack of drooling guys, showing off her exposed midsection and too-tight jeans. Although she's young—just a freshman at a school near Talcott—tonight she looks good.

Gina laughs as the basketballers crudely compliment her moves.

She has no idea what she's starting, Paul thinks as he watches Gina flirt with The Crew. He leans back against the bar, content to just observe the insanity.

Soon, Goldstein and Willett try to grab Gina and dance closely with her, but she backs off.

"Come on, Geeena!" Willett whines.

Gina giggles. "Not so close."

But the guys don't exactly respect her space.

Laughing at his friends, Moyer leans into Paul and whispers, "Watch this!"

Paul frowns, knowing just how far his friend can take things.

Moyer jumps into the fray and, without an ounce of caution, pulls Gina in close.

"Get off me!" Gina yells, pushing Moyer away.

Bad idea.

Paul watches Moyer's expression darken. A vein emerges on his forehead. He's a notoriously bad drunk, prone to fits of sudden anger. Realizing he has to stop this thing before it starts, Paul steps forward to hold Moyer back. But he's too drunk and too late.

Moyer reaches for Gina once again, yanking her in close, making the girl wince in pain.

Paul moves again to defend Gina, but before he can say or do anything, Willett holds him back, pushing him up against the bar. As Paul struggles with Willett, Gina breaks free from Moyer and runs out of Tropixxx.

"Game on!" Moyer yells out as he sets off after her.

Goldstein follows.

"Stop!" Paul tries to shout, but it comes out

a slurred jumble. Willett and Schloss then grab a hold of him and literally drag Paul out of the club. He's too drunk to resist, and his friends are too rowdy to care.

The Crew piles into Goldstein's souped-up Beamer as he screeches to a halt outside the bar. Paul and the others squeeze into the way-too-small car, like five sinister clowns.

Goldstein then takes off, with Moyer riding shotgun, scanning the streets for Gina.

"Gina? Oh, Geeena!" Moyer sings out as the rest of the guys laugh.

Over the jacked-up sound system, Paul protests again: "Leave her alone, Moyer!"

But Moyer's not having it. And neither is Goldstein as the car screeches down the block.

"Like we're going to take *your* advice on women, Paul!" Schloss teases.

Feeling woozy, Paul leans back into his seat. *Got to get my shit together,* he thinks, grabbing his head to relieve that pounding inside.

The Crew then spots Gina running up Second Avenue, wiping tears from her eyes.

"Poor baby!" Goldstein laughs, and he accelerates toward her.

Paul reaches out, sloppily grabs Goldstein's shoulder, but his friend shrugs him off. Then Goldstein guns the car and pulls next to Gina, almost hopping onto the curb with reckless enthusiasm.

Gina jumps back with a horrified scream.

Willett leans out of a window, reaching toward the frightened freshman. "Get in, Gina!" He laughs. "We just want to be friends!"

The boys cackle.

"Stop following me!" she screams, looking up and down the block, probably for help.

"Seriously, guys!" Paul slurs. "She's scared shitless."

"Shut up!" Moyer says, pushing his friend back against the seat.

"We just want to hold hands!" Willett adds as he high-fives Schloss.

"You'd better leave me alone!" Gina cries, trying to squeeze around the vehicle. "My brother's gonna be here any second and he'll kick your asses!"

"Yeah, right!" Moyer screams, fully enjoying

the hunt. "I bet your brother's like ten years old or some shit. If you even *have* a brother," he adds, licking his lips.

"No!" Paul shouts.

Gina picks up the pace. The car lurches forward.

"Guys, stop!" Paul is sobering fast.

But The Crew is just warming up:

"Give us a taste, Gina!"

"This isn't funny!" Paul says.

"I love you, Gina!"

"Enough already! Let her go!" Paul screams out, fighting to grab the wheel.

Goldstein turns around and slams a forearm into Paul's chest. "DO NOT touch my car, dude!" he yells.

Suddenly, Gina breaks for it, crossing the street awkwardly in her stilettos.

Goldstein whips back around, realizing he's losing her, and slams on the accelerator. Everyone laughs again, but then they accidentally hit her. They're shocked silent.

"Holy shit!" Goldstein yells as the car screams to a stop and Gina disappears in front of it.

"What the hell?" Paul shouts, searching

for the lock to his door. He manages to find the lock and throws the door open. *This is not good!* He spills out onto the street and scrambles to stand back up. "Come on!" Paul shouts as he looks back to the car, expecting The Crew to follow. "What?" Paul screams.

They don't get out. They don't even budge! His boys are just sitting there, shocked silent. Four muscle-bound cowards.

Paul turns his head and looks toward the front of the car; he can't see Gina yet, but he can *hear* her moaning.

"Get the fuck out here! We gotta check on her!" Paul insists.

That's when a ghost-white Goldstein slams his car into reverse and takes off.

"COME BACK HERE!" Paul yells out into the night, but his voice just echoes off the buildings.

Now he's all alone.

Shit! he thinks, trying to jog his brain into functioning shape again, then slowly turns toward the moaning. *I hope she just twisted an ankle or something. After all, we weren't going that fast when they bumped her.*

Ready to apologize to Gina, Paul finally looks down at the girl. "No!" he cries out in horror.

Gina is writhing on the concrete in a pool of blood.

15

Blood spills across the

curb in a long stream, finding its way to a nearby storm drain.

Gina's body jerks in frenetic bursts. Her hands reach out to Paul, and she wheezes out a slow, low moan.

"Gina! Can you hear me?" Paul asks. He kneels down and cradles the girl in his arms. *Things are bad. Very bad*, he chants to himself.

"Don't worry, okay? Just . . . stay calm."

Gina just stares at Paul through her tears. She tries to speak, but blood bubbles out from her mouth.

"You'll be okay, Gina. I'll get you help." Paul rips off his jacket and bundles it against the girl's forehead, trying to stop the flow of blood.

It isn't working.

Blood like a river.

Paul breathes out slowly and steadily as he

fishes his cell phone out of his pocket. He imme-diately dials 911, but as he presses "Talk," he notices that the display on his phone is shat-tered—probably from the fight with Steve.

Trying to keep his cool, Paul holds Gina's hand. Her palm is growing cold, lifeless. Her eyes shut as she barely whispers something.

"What did you say, Gina?" Paul asks. "Can you say it again? Just once more? Please!"

But she says nothing. A few more twitches jolt Gina's body, and then she lies still.

This is not happening! Paul collapses inside. *Why did my boys leave me like this?*

Everyone is abandoning me!

Left with no alternative other than all-out yelling, Paul calls out, "HELLO! HELP!" His voice sounds hollow against the concrete landscape. "Somebody fucking *help* me!"

Paul knows that Sixty-first Street is a quiet, sheltered block, but maybe *someone* is within earshot.

No one comes, however. For a while . . .

Paul looks back down at Gina.

Wait! No!

Her chest is still. The wheezing sound has stopped altogether.

SHE'S NOT BREATHING!

"No!" Paul yells in terror. "Gina!"

Paul leans over Gina's body and presses his lips to hers. He took a lifeguarding class in Nantucket the summer before and still remembers the basics.

Pumping Gina's chest, Paul blows air into her lungs, but nothing happens.

Nothing!

Paul wipes blood from his face and hangs his head in utter misery. A stupid joke . . . and now a girl is dead!

He tried . . . he tried to stop their teasing, but not hard enough.

Now it's too late. Too late for Gina.

Too late to help.

Paul's head spins.

Too late for me? My future? Brown?

Too late to do any good . . .

Slowly and unsteadily, with regret echoing in his head, Paul stands up, backs away from Gina, and heads straight for the subway.

Blood never washes out, Paul thinks as he stands in his bathroom, staring at the red splotches on his face, arms, and hands. He scrubs off as much of it as he can, frowns in the mirror, and shuts off the bathroom light.

A girl is dead! Paul closes his eyes and sees her bloody corpse again. He walks toward his bed as tears well in his eyes. "And I left her there . . . ," he whispers, crawling into bed, aching everywhere. He closes his eyes, but the images of Gina and Steve and Carolee loop through his brain. . . .

A girl is dead. . . .

As Paul lies in his bed, staring blankly at the swirling ceiling fan above, he's startled by a knock on his bedroom door.

A heavy knock.

Maybe Paul's dad heard him come in. Usually he just ignores his son's late arrivals, but tonight, for some reason, maybe Kirk Stone was feeling unusually *involved.*

Paul tries to ignore the knocking, but that's when the pounding starts. "What the hell do you want?" Paul shouts out.

No one responds. Just more banging.

Finally Paul gets up, hurries across his room, and yanks open the large oak door.

It's the police! Three cops in uniform, hands resting on the barrels of their guns!

Gina! Paul's mind shouts. *Good-bye college. Good-bye future. Good-bye everything!*

"Paul Stone?" one of the officers asks.

"Yes . . . ," Paul responds. He feels the acid boiling in his stomach. His scrubbed body burns.

"Senior at Talcott, right?" another says.

Paul feels the moisture in his mouth vanish. He tries to speak, but he can't form the words.

And for a split second, he closes his eyes and waits to hear Gina's name.

The first officer pushes past Paul and begins to search his room. The second one follows suit, while the third keeps an eye on Paul, grilling him up and down.

Just say it, Paul thinks. *Tell me why you're here. Say it out loud!*

"Carolee Adams . . . ," the third cop starts.

Paul furrows his brow. *What? Carolee?*

"Your *girlfriend?*" the cop continues, staring at him with hard, focused eyes.

"Yes?" Paul nods his head and relaxes a bit. *Maybe they didn't know about Gina.*

"She's dead."

"Huh? What?" Paul says in a panic, not

sure he heard right. Don't they mean *Gina?*

"We found her in Central Park," the stone-faced cop continued. "Murdered."

"No, but—" Paul is swimming in confusion. He feels vomit welling in his throat.

WHAT THE HELL IS GOING ON?

"Carolee Adams is dead!" the officer shouts.

"No!" Paul screams, anguish twisting his face.

As Paul sinks to his knees, the cop suddenly wrences his arms behind his back and slams handcuffs on his trembling wrists. "And we're arresting you for her murder."

16

"Oh, my God," Kirsten mumbled, her head weary as the early morning light streamed into the kitchen windows of the beach house. *Two girls,* she thought. *Two brutal deaths. . . .*

Thrust back into reality, Kirsten stiffened and pulled farther away from Kyle as she remembered Sam—and how her last moments of life had to have been just as terrifying.

"I did *threaten* Carolee that night, but I didn't *kill* her," Kyle insisted. "The cops found my fingerprints all—"

Kirsten watched him hold back tears and hug himself with his strong arms. She searched his eyes, trying to process it all. Was he telling her the truth? Or was he just a really good actor? She wasn't sure.

"Someone had tied up her hands with . . .

my Talcott tie," he went on. "I must have left it at the bar. It's sick!" Kyle stopped talking and looked away as his tears finally broke through, and he swiped at them with the backs of his hands. And Kirsten had to fight against the instinct to reach out to him.

Maybe he is telling the truth, Kirsten thought.

"My prints were all over her body. Wherever she wasn't . . . cut," Kyle whispered. "And because of our fight at the Zoo and the tie . . . it seemed like an open-and-shut case."

Kirsten shook her head. "But why didn't you tell the *truth*? You had an alibi."

"That's just it," Kyle said. "I went to the guys, and they flat out told me that they wouldn't support me. If they did, they could have been charged with second-degree murder. So my 'friends' let me take the fall. My best friends!" His tears were uncontrollable now.

Kirsten wanted to cry, too, but she didn't. She reached out and touched Kyle's hand.

"My lawyer," Kyle went on, "actually my *dad's* lawyer, said it could be worse if I told the truth. I'd be tried for both crimes! That was the biggest mistake of my life. When my name was released to the papers, Brown revoked my college scholarship. And even though the case hadn't begun, Talcott expelled me for 'tarnishing the school's moral standing in the community' and, worst of all, my *dad* even started doubting me!" His eyes seemed hurt and defeated. "My life was ruined!"

"Calm down, Kyle," she heard herself saying. "It's okay. . . ."

"I couldn't tell the police where I was at the time of Carolee's murder," Kyle went on. "I was directly involved in another death the very same night! God, that *same night.*"

Kirsten had no idea what to think anymore or how to react. She looked down at the kitchen tiles and let out a long, deep breath.

"Believe me, Kirsten." Kyle raised his head, his face stained with tears. "I was ready to own up to what happened to Gina. Take responsibility. But then I realized I'd be killing myself *and* incriminating my friends."

Some friends, Kirsten thought as she looked back at Kyle. He was clearly in pain.

"At least I *thought* they were my friends." Kyle clenched his fists.

"God . . ." Kirsten sighed again. "But if you

didn't do it, who killed her? Who killed Carolee?"

"I don't know, Kirsten." Kyle shook his head. "I guess anyone at the Zoo could have found my tie . . . and used it on Carolee. But why? That's the question I've been asking myself every day for three years. I have to find out what really happened," he said. "That's why I came back to New York—to find out the truth and to clear my name. I can't live with this cloud hanging over my head."

There was a long pause. Kirsten stared into Kyle's eyes, hoping that if she looked at them long enough, she would know the truth— know if Kyle was a murderer, or a victim of circumstance. *Why would he tell such a horrible story if it wasn't true?* she wondered. Then she thought of something else.

"What about the other girls?" Kirsten asked. "What about Sam and Emma?" Maybe Kyle didn't kill Carolee, but that didn't mean he wasn't involved in the other murders.

"I don't know. Have you ever heard of a copycat killer? Someone who imitates another crime? Maybe that's the answer, or maybe the murderer is just a nut who likes to kill pretty girls. . . ." Kyle paused and raked a hand through his wavy brown hair. "Honestly, I don't have the answer . . . not yet," he said. "But I *will* find it. I have to. You don't know what it's like in prison, Kirsten. I can't go back there. Will you help me?"

Kirsten heard the pain in his voice. The pain and confusion. She looked at him, *really* looked at him, for the first time in eight months. He was so thin. Kyle looked as if he had lost twenty pounds since she'd last seen him—*at least.*

Kyle seemed so convincing—his pain and anguish so real. Kirsten found herself *wanting* to believe him. She wanted to fly across the table and comfort him and tell him that everything was going to be okay and that she was going to help him find the real killer, and that after this whole mess was behind them, after the truth was finally clear and out in the open for everyone to see, they'd finally be happy. *But . . .*

"I can't do this," Kirsten said. She couldn't put herself out there again. "I've been through too much. This whole thing . . . I don't know . . . it's . . . it's just too hard," She couldn't look at him.

"Kirsten . . . ," he said. "I need you . . . *please.* You're the only person I've got."

Kirsten's eyes welled up. "It's not fair of you," she told him. "You can't do this to me. It's not fair!"

Kyle nodded. "Okay," he whispered. "I . . . I'll—"

"Just . . . get away," she said. "Run . . . far away. . . . I won't turn you in. I won't tell anybody that you were here. Just get away, before it's too late. Get away before anybody finds you."

Kyle nodded. Just as he was about to say something, the kitchen door flew open.

17

Julie stumbled through the kitchen doorway drenched, drunk, and delighted.

Kirsten glanced back at Kyle and relaxed a little when she realized he had snuck away. She hoped she could keep Julie in the kitchen long enough for Kyle to duck out of the front door.

Kirsten turned back to see Julie dancing around the room, ranting about how she was going to make "canpakes!" She pulled out a large box of Bisquick from the pantry and opened it, covering herself in a cloud of pancake mix. "What's up with you, slut?" Julie asked sloppily.

Kirsten rolled her eyes. Even though Julie was wasted, she could still read Kirsten like a book. "Nothing," she lied.

"This is no time to hold things inside,

Kirrrrsten," Julie said, and cracked a mischievous smile. "Like your *'psychiatrist'* said. What's wrong? Tell Julie *allllll* about it."

"I said *nothing* is wrong," Kirsten snapped, not meaning to.

Julie shrugged. "Whatever." She rambled on about the rest of the party, the joy of pancakes, about how "hot" Clark was, and walked into the hallway bathroom.

Kirsten slumped in her chair by the kitchen table. She stared at the one Kyle had been sitting in not five minutes earlier, and boiled with the truth.

"Ahhhrrrrrrggggggh!" Julie screamed from the bathroom. "Helllllllllp!"

Uh-oh. Kirsten jumped up and ran toward the screaming.

"Ahhhhhhhhh!" Julie rushed out of the bathroom, arms waving above her head, and she slammed right into Kirsten. Both of them toppled to the floor as Kyle fled into the living room, dragging a shower curtain behind him.

"The phone!" Julie scrambled to her feet, making a beeline for the cordless by the couch in the living room.

Kirsten found herself grabbing Julie and

holding her back so that she could get to the phone first.

"What the hell are you doing?" Julie screamed.

"Just wait!" Kirsten pleaded. As the two friends wrestled toward the phone, Kyle bolted out the front door.

Kirsten relaxed as she saw Kyle tear down the circular driveway and leap over Julie's fence.

"Are you crazy!" Julie screamed. "We had him here! Right here in the house!"

"Julie—" Kirsten began.

"We could've turned that psycho in!" Julie continued, and grabbed the phone from Kirsten's hand.

Before she could dial 911, Kirsten snatched the phone from her and backed away.

"Give me that!" Julie yelled, swaying in her drunkenness.

"He didn't do it!" Kirsten blurted out. She raised her hands to her mouth, trying to trap the words back inside.

Julie's face sank. Her arms dropped to her side. "No. You can't be *serious*, Kirsten . . . right?"

"I am," Kirsten replied. "Very serious. He came here to tell me the truth."

"Wait." Julie was stunned. You *knew* he was here? I cannot *believe* you, Kirsten! He could've killed you. . . . He could've killed *me*!"

Kirsten turned bright red. It was true. She *had* risked Julie's life by not warning her. "But . . . he told me what really happened," Kirsten mumbled as guilt and confusion closed in on her.

"And you fell for it," Julie muttered, suddenly sober. "You know, you amaze me more and more, Kirsten. How could you be so *stupid*?"

Stupid? Kirsten thought, finding herself getting angry. "You weren't there," she told Julie. "You didn't hear his story. I did, and he was telling the truth!" she screamed.

Cursing under her breath, Julie stalked into the kitchen. "It figures," she muttered.

"Hey, wait a minute!" Kirsten followed. "What was *that* supposed to mean?"

"Like you're such a good judge of character these days!" Julie replied without looking back.

"I *know* you want to elaborate, Julie,"

Kirsten said. She couldn't stand when Julie got her holier-than-thou attitude. "Go ahead. Say what you've been thinking for months. Say it. Get it off your chest. I want to hear it!"

"Well, first Paul Stone, and now Leslie Fenk?" Julie explained. "You don't exactly have a great track record when it comes to surrounding yourself with quality people, Kirsten. I mean, how many times are you going to fall for this guy's bullshit? And Leslie—do you know what people are saying about you two? That you guys are more than just buddies."

"Oh, come on. You don't believe that. You're just jealous!" Kirsten fought back.

"Of that slut? Yeah, right!" Julie's words cut deep. "You just hang with her so she can get you high! You're pathetic!" Julie spat with finality, turning off the kitchen light, hurrying past Kirsten and going upstairs.

Kirsten felt as if she had been punched in the stomach. And she was about to punch back. She spun around and caught up to Julie on the steps. She grabbed her arm and got directly in her face. "You know what, Julie? I think you're jealous that I'm starting to make new friends," she said.

"Oh, please." Julie rolled her eyes.

"And you are definitely jealous of what Kyle and I had," Kirsten added.

"Yeah, right!" Julie huffed, but there was something in her eyes that told Kirsten she might be right about this one. She went with it.

"I mean, what do *you* know about love? The last guy who liked you—I mean, really *liked* you—was Kenny Dwiggler! In seventh grade!"

Julie's face twisted with pain. She pulled away from Kirsten and ran upstairs.

"All those one-night stands don't count!" Kirsten cried. She knew how to hit where it hurt.

Julie broke into sobs as she slammed her bedroom door.

As she listened to Julie cry, Kirsten felt instantly sorry for what she had just said to her friend. *When did I become such a world-class bitch?* she wondered, but before she had a chance to follow her friend upstairs, Julie swung her door back open again.

"I am so sick of dealing with your *shit*, Kirsten. I've been there for you every day for the last *eight miserable months*, but I can't do it anymore, okay?" she said.

"Julie, I—"

"No. Sam was my friend too!" Julie interrupted. "And you're in love with her *killer?*"

Those words were like a slap. Kirsten sank onto the steps. Intense feelings of shame and anger and fear overwhelmed her.

"I don't want to see you here when I wake up!" Julie shouted before slamming her door again, this time for good.

Kirsten moved to go upstairs again, but then stopped herself. *I'd better let Julie cool down,* she thought. *Nothing I can say—no apology—can fix this right now.*

She gathered her things and opened the door of the Pembrokes' farmhouse.

The sun had risen and was now shining bright above the trees. It was a beautiful morning. Her thoughts turned back to Kyle as she walked across the gravel driveway. His story had sounded so real, so convincing. She wondered where he would go. Where could he run to?

But that didn't matter anymore.

I have to patch things up with Julie, Kirsten thought as she turned up a long, straight road, heading for the Jitney stop in the nearest town. *I can't push away the one true friend I have left. . . .*

18

As Kirsten knocked on the large, stately door of 523 East Seventieth Street on the Upper East Side of Manhattan, she heard Dr. Fitzgerald's voice in her head: "Maybe the best way to get over Sam is to help other people get over Sam."

Sam Byrne lived in a quaint brownstone on Seventieth and Park. The place was some kind of registered historical landmark. Sam was *old money*—the kind of first-generation, *Mayflower* money that afforded you prime real estate in the snobbiest area of Manhattan. Kirsten knocked again and then she just waited, seemingly forever. Just as she turned to leave, the door slowly opened.

Kirsten was surprised to see Sam's stepfather—"Rolf from Düsseldorf," as Sam always called him—staring out from the entryway. The Byrnes' live-in housekeeper, Maria, usually answered the door. And Rolf Knauerhase was not looking his usual personal-trainer handsome self. His wavy, sandy-colored hair was a mess, his piercing blue eyes seemed to have a dull haze over them, and he was dressed in nothing more than a pair of wrinkled pajamas.

"Hi, Rolf," Kirsten said, trying not to grimace. She usually loved talking with him. She and Sam used to always make fun of his German accent, but all in all, he wasn't a bad guy. But today was different. There was a strong smell of whiskey on his breath as he embraced her a little too long.

"So gut to be seeing you, Keersten," he croaked, trying to fix his hair and make himself look more presentable.

"Great to see you, too," she said as Rolf led her inside.

A flash of memories came back to Kirsten as she stepped into the marble foyer: hours of hide-and-go-seek . . . tossing Barbie dolls off the top of Sam's grand staircase . . . the stress of getting ready for their first fall dance at Woodley. . . .

Kirsten glanced up at a white sheet that

was hanging limply over the large painting of the Byrne family that dominated the foyer. "Is Bobbi here?" Kirsten turned back to Rolf, trying her best to smile.

"Um . . . no," Rolf replied, but he didn't sound too convincing.

"Okay . . . ," Kirsten said awkwardly, not knowing exactly what to say. "Um, could I see Sam's room?" she finally asked. "I, um, just want to see it—like, for a minute."

"Sure," Rolf said, his eyes surprisingly sad at the mention of his stepdaughter's name.

Kirsten was blown away by how affected Rolf was. She was so wrapped up in her own sadness that she nearly forgot that other people missed Sam too. Rolf pointed the way up to Sam's room—a way that Kirsten knew well— and shuffled off toward the kitchen.

Wow, Kirsten thought. If Rolf was leveled by Sam's death, she could only imagine what Sam's mom, Bobbi, must be going though.

I should have come to see them sooner, Kirsten thought. She felt selfish as she walked up to Sam's third-floor bedroom. She hadn't been thinking about anyone but herself for a long time.

The door to Sam's bedroom was already halfway open, and Kirsten quietly entered it. The room clearly hadn't been touched since Sam's murder. Books lay everywhere, makeup lined the windowsill, and Sam's iMac was framed with pictures of the Three Amigas. There were even a few outfits tossed casually across the bed—rejects for their big night out at the Party Room.

The last night at the Party Room.

She burst into tears. Being back in Spammie's room brought a tide of emotions. She noticed Sam's well-worn copy of *Leaves of Grass* sticking out from under a pillow on her bed—the book that she and Sam had read with religious fervor. Kirsten found herself smiling, and she wiped away her tears. As she picked up the book, several papers fell out of it. Notes or something.

Curious, Kirsten unfolded one and started to read it. It was a "To Do" list.

1) Bio: Chapters 3-5
2) Cal—study!!!
3) Peer Leadership meeting w/ Dean K. @ Wood
4) Yoga w/ Jules and Kirsten!

Kirsten smiled at Sam's manic handwriting. She remembered how simple their lives used to be. At one point, they were both just normal high school girls, living normal high school lives. It was nice to have these memories. Good memories.

"You okay, Kirsten?" a weary voice said from behind her.

Kirsten jumped back, flustered by the sudden interruption. She quickly slipped the book and notes into her Coach tote and turned around.

Oh, my God, Kirsten thought when she saw Sam's mom standing in the doorway. The woman who had been like Kirsten's second mother now seemed like a total stranger. She was a rail. A skeleton, almost. Bobbi's hair was dull and gray. Her skin looked flaky and raw without her usual makeup. "Hi . . . um, Bobbi," Kirsten started nervously.

"Please stay as long as you like, Kirsten," Bobbi said. "I'm glad you're here." She looked lifeless without her daughter. She looked lost.

"I am so sorry I didn't come sooner. I . . . I—" Kirsten felt herself starting to cry again.

She didn't want to, but the moment was just too intense.

"I am too," Bobbi said sadly, looking over Sam's room. "She was . . ."

"Incredible," Kirsten finished her sentence. "She was the greatest friend you could ever ask for."

"And daughter," Bobbi agreed softly, sitting down on the edge of the bed.

Kirsten reached out and put her hand on Bobbi's shoulder. And if a smile can be defined as an infinitesimal rising of the corners of one's mouth, Sam's mom smiled.

Then Kirsten let out a long breath she hadn't even realized she was holding. And she stood there, holding Bobbi's shoulder, letting the tears come, and wishing that she had visited a long time ago.

Later that day, Kirsten was sprawled out on her canopy bed and reading the notes that she had carefully laid out on her duvet. *Leaves of Grass* had practically burned a hole in her purse while she was sitting in Bobbi Byrne's library drinking tea and trading memories about Sam. She didn't know why she took the book, but Kirsten had been dying to sift through the notes she had found.

Now, reading the miscellaneous flirtations and gossip and lists, Kirsten felt as if she were with her friend again. She even found herself laughing out loud.

God, I miss you! she thought as she read and read and read. Sam not only had notes she had received, but ones she had written herself.

Kirsten scanned through a series of back-and-forths between herself and Sam from when they were in Mr. Costas's bio class together, then she saw a few notes between Sam and Brandon.

As Kirsten unfolded another paper, she remembered how Sam had broken up with Brandon and how badly he had taken it. And how terrible Brandon had looked just a few nights ago. Then she read the note:

Brandon—

I saw Jones again. I had to. I know you'll be angry w/ me, but I had to. I have to keep seeing him. I just have to.

Kirsten furrowed her brows. *Sam never*

mentioned any Jones guy to me. She rushed through the rest of the note. She couldn't believe what she was reading. Apparently Sam was seeing this Jones guy on the side. And Brandon knew about it! *How come Sam never said anything about it?*

She scanned the next note:

I can't go on like this. It's got to stop, Brandon. Don't go to Volume again, please. I'm telling you for your own good. Stay away from Jones. He's really pissed and I don't think I can control the situation anymore. It's major. Trust me, this isn't like at Talcott, B. Just do me a favor and keep your butt OUT of VOLUME!!! Okay?

Kirsten read the last two notes again. Although the scraps of information that she could pick out were sketchy at best, she felt as if she was seeing a whole new chapter of Sam's life. Kirsten had never heard of this Jones guy. Volume? Was it a bar? Kirsten had never been there.

Kirsten wondered if this had something to do with why Sam broke up with Brandon. Now that Kirsten thought about it, Sam had never actually said why she'd dumped him. What did she mean—"This is major"?

Kirsten couldn't make out the story, but something had been going on between Sam and Brandon right up to the day Sam broke up with him, and maybe the night she disappeared!

Who is Jones? Why didn't Sam tell her about him?

The warm feelings of nostalgia drained out of Kirsten as she realized that her best friend— her *sister,* practically—had kept a secret from her. By the looks of it, an *enormous* secret.

"What a total mind game," Scott said the next day as he examined the fractured face of Mademoiselle de Avignon at the Museum of Modern Art.

"That's one way to describe it." Kirsten tilted her head and squinted at the huge Picasso painting.

"It's like he's looking at people through some kind of kaleidoscope or something," Scott added.

"Either that or he was on some heavy drugs," Kirsten joked. She smiled at Scott, glad that he had agreed to hang out with her that day. Julie was still way too angry to speak to, and Kirsten needed to chill with a friend, so she'd called Scott.

As they moved to another of MOMA's permanent collections, however, Kirsten grew quiet. Even though she was having fun with Scott, she couldn't get her mind off the weird notes Sam had written about Jones. She wanted to talk to Julie about them, but of course that wasn't happening anytime soon. And what was Kirsten going to do about that, too?

"You all right, Kirsten?" Scott asked, breaking the silence.

"Huh?" Kirsten replied.

"I said, Are you cool?" Scott led her into another room of paintings. This time they stopped in front of a Magritte—the one with the dark house and the light sky. Scott pushed further. "You can tell me anything—you know that, right?" he said, putting an arm around her shoulders like a comforting brother. "You know, bartenders are practically therapists."

"Is it that obvious I'm upset?" Kirsten asked, smiling weakly.

Scott nodded. "Kind of," he said. "What's going on?"

"Well, Doctor . . ." Kirsten took in a deep breath, and everything spilled out. She told Scott all about the huge disaster in the Hamptons. Her embarrassment with Brian at that party . . . driving home and almost getting into an accident . . . and the huge fight she'd had with Julie the next morning.

"Man," Scott said. "That sucks."

"I know," Kirsten said flatly. "Julie was so mad at me, and we were so mean to each other. But I was worse than Julie was. Much worse. I didn't know I had it in me."

"But what *started* it all?" Scott asked. "What was Julie so mad about?"

Should I tell him about Kyle? Kirsten wondered. But then again, she knew that she could trust him. Scott had been a big support for her ever since Sam died. And one thing that she had always appreciated about him was that he never judged her. Never rolled his eyes when she freaked out over something insignificant . . . never told her she was imagining things, like her other friends had. . . .

"You don't have to tell me if you don't want to," Scott said.

But Kirsten realized that she did want to. She wanted to talk to someone objective. "Kyle came to see me," she finally admitted, staring deeper into the painting in front of them, getting lost in the bright blues and whites. "Out at Julie's beach house."

"Jesus . . . ," Scott said.

"And I think . . ." Kirsten hesitated. "He told me this story, and . . . well . . . I think he might be innocent."

Scott swallowed. "How come?"

Thank God for Scott, Kirsten thought. She appreciated the fact that he was keeping an open mind. But she knew that couldn't tell Scott about Kyle's secret—about what had happened to that girl Gina. Not yet. Not until she knew more.

"I—I just do." She turned her head away from him as they walked on to a Mondrian painting—tiny squares dancing around in a never-ending maze. Then Scott completely surprised her.

"Maybe you're right," he said. "I mean, if this guy was *really* a killer—and he wanted to kill you . . . he had the perfect shot out there at Julie's. But he didn't do it, right?"

Sam smiled at Scott. "Exactly."

"But if Kyle's innocent, who's guilty?" Scott asked.

"I don't know," Kirsten murmured as she ran through all the possible scenarios. If Kyle truly *was* innocent, then who would have had the motive to kill Sam? And, when you thought about it, Kyle didn't have a reason to kill Sam, either, but the police were very willing to blame him for it—maybe it *was* a copycat, as Kyle had said.

Scott put his arm around Kirsten again and drew her in close, making her feel safe. He was strong, protective, and kind. Kirsten was so lucky to have him as a friend. "If we could just think of who else might have a reason to do it. . . ." He sighed, exasperated. "I wish I could talk to Kyle. Maybe I could help you guys figure it out."

"Too bad you can't. I told him to get out of town. He's probably long gone by now. So, I guess we'll never know what happened." Kirsten said, but her mind kept thinking about it—going back to the last night at the Party

Room. *Who was there? Who was there?* She kept asking herself.

There was Kirsten, and Julie, Carla and Sarah, Emma . . . and almost every senior from Woodley. Scott was at the bar . . . Kyle later admitted he was at the Party Room that night . . . and Brandon was there, too, of course. Kirsten remembered he was acting like a jerk and trying to take pictures up Sam's skirt. But Sam just ignored him, and then she met this guy . . . an older guy with reddish hair.

"Eric the Red!" Kirsten yelled out her nickname for the guy. "I've completely forgotten about him. The one who left that night with Sam! Remember? He was cute, but very dangerous looking." Kirsten rambled, reminding Scott about the details of Sam's disappearance. "He turned out to be a dealer named Jones. I found him, and when I asked him about Sam, he freaked out and ran. The police forgot all about him when the evidence pointed to Kyle—and so did I! But that guy is probably long-gone too." And Kirsten wasn't sorry about that. This guy was very shady— and he wasn't happy about her having tracked him down.

"Wait, who?" Scott squinted as he thought of something. Then a flash of recognition: "Did this guy have *red* hair like Seth Green?"

Kirsten nodded. "Uh-huh."

"Oh, my God, Kirsten!" Scott said. "I remember him . . . and . . . and . . . I saw him last night at a place called Volume!"

19

"'I saw him last night at a place called Volume!'" Scott's words echoed in Kirsten's mind the next day as she poured a few of Leslie's pills into her hand. She popped them into her mouth and leaned over the faucet in the WXRJ bathroom. Kirsten drank greedily and swallowed them down.

So I can concentrate . . . focus, she chanted to herself. She hadn't been able to sleep all night.

As Kirsten straightened, she splashed a handful of water on her face and tried to shake off her thoughts. Now she wished that she hadn't told Kyle to leave town. She needed to find him somehow—to talk about that guy Sam left with. But right now she had to work.

After a few more minutes of deep breathing, Kirsten walked out of the ladies' room and down the hallway toward Studio Five. When Kirsten entered the studio, she was shocked to see Kate Grisholm already there, throwing mini-disks all over the tech room.

"There you are, Kirsten!" Kate said, exasperated.

Uh-oh, Kirsten thought. *I must've lost track of time in the bathroom.* She looked down at her watch. "Sorry, I—"

Kate raised a hand to stop her. "You know, when you first came here, I thought you were going to be my star intern, but now . . . what's going on with you?"

"I . . . ah—" Kirsten stopped short. She had nothing to say to defend herself. She'd been doing an awful job lately, and she knew it.

"I had to come in *two hours* early today to reorganize this place. You left it a total mess on Friday!"

"I'm sorry," Kirsten mumbled, her hands beginning to shake. *Maybe I should have taken three instead of four pills this morning,* she thought.

"There are *a lot* of people who would gladly take this job!" Kate said as she rose from Kirsten's chair.

"I'll do better. I promise!" Kirsten pleaded as Kate stormed off toward the main studio, leaving Kirsten to file the rest of the mini-disks by herself.

Before she closed the tech room door, Kate shot Kirsten an icy glance.

A warning.

Kirsten knew she was hanging on to this job by a thread. Only minutes remained before *Love Stinks* would begin. There was no way Kirsten could get all the work done.

"Good morning, sunshine!" Brian smiled, swinging open the door to the studio.

"Is it?" Kirsten said flatly, shoveling mini-disks into random piles.

Brian bent down and immediately started helping Kirsten. "Looks like you and Kate are best friends now," he joked, trying to lighten the mood.

Kirsten laughed and nudged him with her arm. "Thanks."

Then, with blinding speed, Kirsten filed the last DAT and got ready to man the phones for the show. When a still-frustrated Kate Grisholm took her seat in front of the main headset, Kirsten was ready to give her a thumbs-up.

The engineer cued the intro music, and the

show buzzed to life. Kirsten exhaled and smiled. She *loved* her job. She couldn't stand the thought of losing this opportunity.

As she finished her prep work, Brian just looked on in admiration. "Know what, Kirsten?" he said. "When you're actually *here*, you really kick ass at this!"

"Thanks," Kirsten said, taking in the compliment. But she had to explain. "I've just had a lot on my mind recently."

She remembered the rainy night. Their conversation outside Julie's. How she had turned Brian down. How he had taken it so well.

"It's all right, Kirsten," he assured her. "I know all about it."

Huh? Kirsten stopped working suddenly. "Know all about *what?*" she asked, afraid to hear the answer. Why should he be bothered with the madness of her life?

"Well," Brian began. "I ran into some tweaked-out guy named Brandon last night while I was bar hopping with a few friends. He told me about the, um, *murders.* And about your old boyfriend."

No! Kirsten's mind screamed. Brandon

Yardley kept finding ways to mess with her life. She knew she should talk to him about that Jones guy, but Kirsten didn't want to go there with him. "Listen to me, Brian," Kirsten snapped. "Brandon Yardley is psycho. Seriously. Don't believe a word—"

The phone rang.

The first caller! Kirsten remembered. She was getting distracted again. She had to focus. She couldn't afford another mess-up!

Before Kirsten could answer the phone, Brian picked it up. "*Love Stinks*," he said, winking at Kirsten. "It's for you." he said, handing the phone to her.

For me? Kirsten thought. A sudden shiver ran up her spine. *Is it Kyle? Did he call me again? I want to talk, but how am I going to explain the call to Kate?*

See you later, Brian mouthed as Kirsten turned to her work. Brian then turned to leave. He'd been gone from the mail room for *way* too long.

"*Love Stinks*," Kirsten repeated into the phone.

"You can say that again, baby!"

Not Kyle, Kirsten realized. *Leslie Fenk.*

"Hey, sexy!" Leslie sang into the receiver, a sultry R&B song whispering in the background.

"Leslie, you can't call me on this number," Kirsten whispered, ducking out of Kate's line of sight. "Why didn't you use my cell phone?"

"I will next time, okay?" Leslie said. Then she started to giggle. "Stop that, Danny!" she whispered to someone in the room. She was calling to invite Kirsten and a guest to a party she was hosting that very night in the super-chic meatpacking district.

After a pause, Kirsten decided to go. She knew she should really go check out that bar where Scott saw "Eric the Red." But Kirsten decided to blow it off. She needed to relax more than ever. "I'm in," she said.

"Good. Don't forget to wear something trasheee!" was the last thing Leslie cooed before she screamed and laughed and hung up the phone.

She might be crazy, but at least she's fun, Kirsten thought. *And a party is just what I need. But who would want to go with me to a Leslie Fenk party? Definitely not Julie.* She glanced out the window of Studio Five and spotted Brian depositing mail in the station manager's in box and got her answer.

"I had no idea it was going to be like this," Kirsten whispered to Brian as they passed a sign that said WELCOME TO LESLIE FENK'S WONDER-FUL WORLD OF SEX PARTY! Then a sign that listed a set of do's and don'ts for the party, such as: "Do feel free to get naked at any time within the course of the evening," and "Don't feel as if you have to take part in the action—some people just like to watch."

Brian didn't say anything as he gaped around while they entered the dimly lit loft on Little West Twelfth Street.

Kirsten was embarrassed, to say the least, and she was going to kill Leslie just as soon as she could find her! The girl had conveniently left out the part about this being an X-rated theme-park party in her invite.

She took in the scene. Strobe lights. Incense. Velvet-covered couches. A group of scantily clad blondes standing by a curtain of metal beads, smoking skinny cigarettes and pretending to look unaffected by the scene.

There's sheer, and then there's topless, Kirsten

thought as she watched them practically devour Brian with their eyes while they walked by them.

"Ooh, he's delicious," one girl said, licking her bloodred lips and staring directly at Brian.

"Mmm . . . ," another one, reaching out and grazing her fingers across the front of his black Armani T-shirt.

"Uh, *excuse* you!" Kirsten pulled the slut brigade off her dazed but not *entirely* upset date as they walked through a curtain of metal beads and found themselves in a completely foreign environment: trip-hop blared loudly from invisible speakers, and kids on Ecstasy lay in corners of a large, cushioned room.

"I'm sorry." Kirsten turned to Brian, but before he had a chance to respond, someone grabbed Kirsten's butt! Hard! "Hey!" she shouted, and spun around.

It was Leslie, dressed to maim severely in shiny leather pants and a Gaultier bustier, and looking completely gone on something. "Hello, my pretties!" Leslie yelled, even though she was hugging both Kirsten and Brian already. "Welcome to my naughty little fiesta!"

"Thanks," Kirsten began. "And I brought—"

Before Kirsten could even finish her sentence, however, Leslie's tongue was halfway down Brian's throat. Kirsten frowned. *Thanks a lot, Leslie!*

"Don't be so naive!" Kirsten could hear Julie's voice now, mocking her and being 100 percent right.

When Leslie and Brian finally separated, Brian turned to Kirsten with a surprising smile. He didn't mind! He hadn't minded *at* all.

"What the hell are you doing, Brian?" Kirsten cried.

But Brian's expression changed. "Sometimes you gotta just go with the flow," he murmured.

"Come on, Kirsten. Don't be so uptight," Leslie cooed. "I'm sure there's plenty of Brian to go around. Want to see?"

Kirsten's stomach turned. "I don't think so," she said.

"Leslie wants to see . . . Leslie like-y," she purred, dragging her new boy toy away.

So that's it, huh? Kirsten shook her head in disbelief. That was the cost to enter the Leslie

Fenk Club: one perfect male for the sacrifice. *Well, once a Woodley Bitch, always a Woodley Bitch.* She held her purse tight and walked up to a stainless-steel bar in the far corner of the party. She'd have one drink, and then she was out of there.

As Kirsten ordered and finished her drink in one fluid motion, she thought back to her fight with Julie. More than ever, she wished it had never happened. She had been such a *maniac* that night. Now she needed a real friend. A true friend.

Kirsten wrestled her cell phone out of her too-small purse and speed-dialed her friend. *Please pick up, please pick up,* she chanted to herself as the phone rang.

Straight to voice mail.

Julie was still screening Kirsten's calls.

"Julie. It's me!" Kirsten knew she sounded desperate, but she didn't care anymore. "I'm sooooo sorry, girl. I'm a total bitch, and I—"

Suddenly, a tall, model-esque girl ran a hand across Kirsten's face, dusting her with glitter.

Kirsten whipped around, startled. She hung up the phone and shouted, "Can I help you?"

"Hi there." The girl leaned in close to Kirsten's face. "You're really pretty."

"No offense, but that's not my thing." Kirsten pushed the girl away from her—a little too hard. The waif-ish model skittered across the floor, sailing into a pack of older guys.

Kirsten looked around for Brian, who was nowhere to be seen. People groped one another everywhere, grinding in corners, French kissing on the dance floor. Freaked and suddenly claustrophobic, she ran out of the loft as fast as she could!

"Taxi!" she screamed as she hit the street. She tried to calm down now that she was outside, but she noticed that everyone in line for Leslie's party was gawking at her.

Why is everyone looking at me? she wondered, looking down at her outfit: Just a simple black French Connection miniskirt, a Scoop tank top, and a pair of strappy Manolos. *What are you staring at?* Kirsten wanted to scream. *This city is crazy,* she thought as she flagged down a passing livery cab. *And Brian's another lost cause.*

Kirsten climbed inside and gave the driver

her address. It was definitely time to go home.

As the cab raced uptown, jostling Kirsten from side to side, she sank into the backseat and wondered how she had ever gotten involved with Leslie Fenk. Julie had been so right about the girl. And now, Kirsten wished more than anything that she could have her best friend by her side. She missed Julie . . . and she missed Sam, too.

"Why couldn't it just go back to the way it was!" she screamed out the open window. "Why do there have to be so many freaks in this city!" she said, ignoring the odd look the driver was giving her.

Then she sat back and watched the city blur by. It was never going to go back to the way it was, she realized. Julie might never forgive her and, well, Sam was gone. And though Kirsten wished she had the power to make that not so, she knew she could do nothing to change it.

There was only one thing that she *could* do. Now that she believed Kyle was innocent, there was a killer out there. Sam's killer. Someone who had gotten away with murder. Maybe if she could find out who he is—she'd be able to move on. To make this awful time in her life just a bad memory.

But she had to decide on one thing first. *No more pills. No more booze,* Kirsten thought. *Just the truth.* She had avoided things for far too long.

Just as she had resolved herself to action, the cab raced by a brightly lit bar. She couldn't believe her eyes. The sign outside said VOLUME in small neon letters.

Volume! That's it! Kirsten remembered. Volume was the bar she had read about in Sam's letter! *The one where Jones was hanging out.*

"Stop!" Kirsten heard herself scream. The cabbie immediately slammed on the brakes. She paid him and rushed out onto the street. *To do what?* Kirsten asked herself. She didn't have a plan. She just *knew* that she had to find Jones.

He'd have answers. He had to.

Taking in a deep breath, mixing courage with craziness, Kirsten walked under the neon sign and entered Volume.

The place was a dive in every sense of the word. The walls were lined with peeling yellow wallpaper. There was no top shelf behind the bar. Even though the ban on smoking had been on for over a year, Volume smelled like an ashtray. A couple of junkies congregated near the back bathrooms, looking for a fix. And that was about it.

"Drinking or just looking?" someone muttered behind Kirsten.

Kirsten spun around to find herself face-to-face with a female bartender. She was an Amazon: well over six feet tall, wearing heavy gauge earrings and an alligator-skin choker. The bartender had a tattoo of a small black spider under the corner of her right eye.

Kirsten gulped down her fear. Maybe running into a random bar at one in the morning wasn't such a great idea. . . .

The black spider danced as the bartender repeated her question: "Drinking or just *looking?*"

"Jones," was the very first thing out of Kirsten's mouth.

Did I just say that? Kirsten yelled to herself in disbelief. She was in total blurt mode, when nothing could stay in her subconscious for more than a few seconds.

Just as Kirsten was about to hurry out, the

Amazon spoke again. "Jones doesn't operate here anymore," she said curtly, strangling a bottle of Seagram's.

Kirsten skin burned with excitement . . . and a little fear. *She knows Jones! But what did she mean by "operate"?*

The bartender stared at her suspiciously, and Kirsten tried to conceal her emotions by biting her upper lip. Inside, however, she was crawling with questions. "Is Jones a dealer?" she burst out again.

The bartender's expression changed: It turned darker, angrier. "Are you *crazy*?"

"Um, well . . . I, uh . . ." Kirsten's mind raced for something to say.

"Look, little girl!" The Amazon marched out from behind the bar to confront Kirsten. "I don't know *who* you are, but I suggest that you take your designer outfit out of here!"

Kirsten froze. She needed to know more, but she also wanted to get out of Volume alive. She just stared at the bartender. "I was just wondering if—"

"I SAID GET THE HELL OUT OF HERE!" the woman screamed, waving to a gigantic bouncer near the door.

Rocking back on her heels, Kirsten knocked over a stool. As she heard the bouncer running toward her from behind, she slipped past the Amazon, avoided a skanky drunk, and ran out of Volume. Just in time to avoid being *thrown* out.

Back outside, Kirsten caught her breath and tried to gather her thoughts: Jones had clearly worked—or *operated*—at Volume. He must've been a dealer there or something, Kirsten assumed. Then her stomach soured. What was Sam doing, going out with a dealer? She had been crazy and liked to party, but not *that* much.

"Looking for Jones, huh?" a voice muttered. Suddenly, *somehow*, a short, skinny man had materialized right next to her. He stared at her jeans skirt, eyes darting from side to side. "You looking for Jones?" he repeated under his breath, drawing closer to her.

Ew. *Too close.* He stunk like a brewery, and need a shower big-time.

"Yeah," Kirsten said as she backed up a little and folded her arms across her chest. She stood tall and tried to look as tall and as confident as possible.

She knew she was in way over her head, but she had to continue.

"I—I—I know where you can f-f-find him," the small man whispered mysteriously. He then looked down the street and waited. And waited. And waited.

After far too long, Kirsten suddenly realized what he was waiting for: money. Cold, hard cash. If she wanted more info, she'd have to pay for it.

Kirsten reached into her purse, pulled out her wallet, and stuffed a twenty into his shaking hands.

"He's at Stop Light tonight. It's a club. Three blocks up, on Tenth Avenue," the skinny man rattled. "Bouncers in the back room. Tell 'em you're on 'the Guest List.'" And with that, he scuffled off down the street and around the corner.

Kirsten shook her head back into clarity and exhaled slowly. She had a choice to make—possibly even a life-or-death choice. She could track down Jones right now and try to solve the mystery, or she could go home to safety. But she would risk never finding Jones again.

Screw it! Kirsten decided. *I'm going.*

She fished her cell phone out of her purse and called Julie one more time. One last time. Kirsten needed her friend now more than ever. The phone rang four times and then went straight to voice mail again.

"Hey! It's Julie P.!" the message started. "Your favorite person in the whole entire world! Please leave a message at the—"

BEEEEEEP.

Kirsten swallowed and spoke in a hushed tone: "Julie. It's Kirsten. I need your help. Seriously. Tonight, if you can. Please. At the Stop Light. Tenth and like Thirty-sixth. Okay? See you there." *What are you doing, Kirsten?* she thought, clicking her phone shut. *Julie's not going to all of a sudden forgive you and show up because you said "please." The way things are going, she probably won't ever talk to you again!*

She sighed and checked out the street toward Stop Light. At this time of night, this part of Tenth Avenue was dark and empty, aside from the occasional staggering drunk. Disregarding a whistle coming from a dark archway across Tenth Avenue, Kirsten held her purse tightly and set off.

She walked quickly up the three blocks to Stop Light. As she hurried, she passed empty storefronts and cheap diners, shuffling homeless men and walls of black garbage bags lining the curbs. Kirsten shivered as she looked across the Midtown wasteland.

When Kirsten arrived at the club, she paused and stood outside for a moment. Now that she was actually there, what the hell was she supposed to do? She took a few seconds to come up with a plan. She'd go to the back room and see if she could find him.

What sort of guy would Sam hide from me? she asked herself as she entered the place, passing a sleeping bouncer. Once inside, Kirsten squinted to adjust her vision. It was dark in there, and she barely made out a bar lining one wall, a collection of weird photographs on the other—faces, limbs, feet—and a small linoleum dance floor in the back. A huge working stoplight illuminated the dazed pupils of the few scattered regulars who were staring at her.

"Excuse me," Kirsten said politely as she stepped around a man swaying near the bar, literally crying into his beer.

She walked toward the back room, scanning the place for someone who looked like a dealer. Everyone was pretty much sloshed and silently slumped in their own worlds. People seemed to be moving in slow motion.

As she walked farther and farther into the club, Kirsten felt a dull tremor overtake her body. She couldn't quite place it, but something was wrong with this place. She had a bad feeling. Really bad. What was wrong with her? She shouldn't be alone in a place like this. Maybe she should get out of there.

Before Kirsten could turn around to leave, she heard a word. One simple word that changed the course of everything:

"Jones."

Jones! Kirsten silently shouted as she twisted back around. *Was someone talking about him? To him? Was Jones there at that moment?* Kirsten shook with fear as she looked around the bar.

Through the darkness and intermittent flashing lights, Kirsten could make out what looked like a drug deal going down near the back exit. A guy who was facing the back door was handing a small plastic bag to a chattering woman. "Jones, Jones, Jones!" she repeated over and over, rubbing her hands on a greasy pair of jeans.

Then the woman raced past Kirsten and into a nearby bathroom. The dealer shook his head and turned around.

Kirsten's knees buckled and she dropped to the floor when she saw his face. . . .

Saw his red, flaming hair.

20

Jones is the red-haired

guy. The last person to see Sam alive. He is Sam's killer! Kirsten screamed inside. She picked herself up from the grimy floor and scrambled backward. Then, a hand grabbed her shoulder!

In a desperate panic, Kirsten looked up. It was only an elderly man staring down at her, looking concerned.

"You all right, little lady?" he slurred through a toothless grin.

Kirsten shot up to her feet and pushed by the elderly man—no time for thank-yous—and ran out of Stop Light.

On the way out, Kirsten ran directly into the bouncer. He was clearly awake now. Before the huge doorman could fully grab her by the wrist, however, Kirsten wrenched free and tore uptown.

I have to tell someone! Kirsten said to herself,

supercharged with adrenaline. She reached for her cell again and immediately called Scott at the Party Room.

"I saw him!" Kirsten yelled as soon as Scott answered the phone.

"Who?" Scott shot back, clearly recognizing the terror in his friend's voice.

"The red-haired guy! His name is Jones!" she screamed as she ran though screaming traffic.

"Jesus, Kirsten!" Scott yelled back. "You can't catch him alone! Who the hell do you think you are?" Kirsten could hear the Party Room buzzing on the other end of the line.

"But—"

"But nothing! That guy is a killer, Kirsten! Get the hell out of there and call the cops!" Scott demanded.

"Okay!" Kirsten hung up and tracked down a yellow taxi waiting at the corner of Thirty-eighth Street and Tenth Avenue. She swung the door open and slid inside, not even looking back to see if Jones was on her trail.

Then, in her second cab of the night, Kirsten sank back into the torn seats and calmed herself. Remembering Scott's advice,

Kirsten picked up her phone again and dialed a different number. This time, Detective Peterson answered.

"Did he see you?" Peterson asked in his clipped, official tone after listening to her.

"I don't *think* so," Kirsten answered, watching the Upper East Side whiz by outside.

"Are you sure?"

"Well, not totally," Kirsten admitted. "Everything happened so quickly. He *might've* seen me . . . but I don't think so." *What was I thinking?* Kirsten said to herself. She could still see Jones's terrible, menacing face.

"Stop Light is *not* the place for a high school girl," Peterson spoke firmly.

"I know that, but I had to do *something!*" Kirsten snapped back.

"No!" Peterson was now shouting into the phone. "That's our job! That's my job! I just want you to go home now. Do you hear me?"

"But don't you need me to I.D. him or something?" She wanted to stay involved.

"No thanks, Kirsten, We'll handle this thing. We've got a file on this Jones guy and we'll get him," Peterson assured her. "Until then, just go home and—"

"I'm already there," Kirsten said as her taxi pulled up in front of her apartment. She paid the cabbie and walked quickly into her lobby.

"If we need your help, we'll call you, okay?" Peterson said. "Kirsten?"

"Yes?" she asked.

"Don't worry about this guy," he said. "We'll get him."

"Finally." Kate Grisholm stuck her head into the tech room, surprising Kirsten as she cued the *Love Stinks* outtro music.

What now? Kirsten frowned, turning toward her boss. She'd been trying her hardest all day. Sweat clung to Kirsten's body even though air-conditioning pumped through WXRJ. "I'm sorry?" she asked tentatively, trying to smile at Kate.

But then a smile spread across her boss's face. "Finally, the *real* Kirsten Sawyer is back!"

"Oh!" Kirsten breathed a sigh of relief.

"Great work out there today," Kate added. "Really. You nailed it. You handled the callers beautifully, and hey, you even saved my butt when I accidentally hung up on the guy with the stocking fetish!"

Kirsten beamed. It felt good to do something *right* for a change.

"Thanks," was all Kirsten could say, relaxing back into her chair.

"No. Thank *you*." Kate smiled, shutting the door. She turned off the overhead lights in the main room, gave Kirsten a final friendly wink and walked out of Studio Five.

Kirsten felt tears welling inside, but this time they were different. They accompanied a deep feeling of accomplishment. True to her promise, Kirsten had managed to stay off drugs for two days now. And she hadn't had a drop to drink, and she had even stopped taking the sleeping medication her psychiatrist had prescribed for her.

As Kirsten smiled to herself, she caught Brian passing by the tech room door. "Brian!" she called out.

No response.

Kirsten frowned curiously and hurried out of her chair. She hadn't seen Brian since the whole Leslie Fenk incident and she was *dying* to ask him about it. "Hey! Brian!" she called out again as she swung the door open.

As she stepped into the hallway, however, Kirsten saw Brian practically *running* away! Even from at least ten yards away, Kirsten could make out a purple ring of hickeys around Brian's neck!

She laughed out loud. *Guess he's not in the sharing mood,* she thought, turning back to close up the studio. As Kirsten locked all the doors and walked down the long WXRJ hallway, she smiled again. It had been a tough workday, and now all she really wanted to do was get a long night's rest. She planned on staying in, curling up to bad TV and, of course, a cup of Mom's cocoa. Her parents were off antiquing Upstate again, but she found herself craving her mother's famous cure-all.

Kirsten rode the elevator down and strolled out of the lobby. She grinned when she caught herself whistling. *I'm whistling while I work!* Kirsten laughed again. *How cheesy!*

As she walked out into the busy Times Square traffic and headed to the subway, an elderly woman approached her. "Got some change?" the woman rasped, scratching the back of her neck.

Usually oblivious to street people, Kirsten stopped and actually *looked* at this woman. She was pulling a shopping cart down the sidewalk, singing to a grimy collection of teddy bears. "Sure." Kirsten smiled.

Although she only had a few teeth in her mouth, the old woman managed a smile back. "Don't worry, be happy!" the woman sang as Kirsten reached for her wallet. She had a fragile, sweet voice.

Don't worry, be happy, Kirsten thought. *Good advice.* But as she handed the woman a few dollars, something flashed into the corner of her eye.

A tie-dyed shirt.

Kirsten accidentally dropped the money on the ground and she turned to face the distraction. Down the block, across the way, Kirsten saw someone jump through a shadow. Advancing.

Was it Jones? He'd been wearing a tie-dyed Phish shirt the night Sam was murdered. Kirsten's heart pounded, and she felt her body suddenly stiffen, her happy mood deflate.

"You all right, sweetie?" the homeless

woman asked as she gathered Kirsten's donation from the sidewalk.

Kirsten couldn't speak. She scanned the streets for Jones. *Is my mind just playing tricks on me again?* she wondered. Then she saw the figure again. Coming closer!

"Hey! Get out of here!" someone shouted behind Kirsten. "You're not wanted here!"

Kirsten turned her head just enough to see Noel, one of the doormen at WXRJ, coming over to shoo away the homeless woman.

"Was she bothering you?" Noel then asked, noticing Kirsten's grave expression.

"No, not at all," she said, distracted, but relieved that Noel had shown up.

Down the street, making his way through broad daylight, Jones was running away.

Kirsten sat in the Seventy-ninth Precinct waiting room, holding her breath against the foul smell of urine that wafted up from the holding pens. Her heart was still racing.

Not even an hour ago, Jones had been tracking her—waiting for just the right moment to take her out.

Peterson finally popped out of his office,

shirtsleeves rolled up, eyes sunken with fatigue. "All right, Kirsten," he said, waving her inside.

Kirsten stood up, still a little shaky, and followed the young detective inside. She sat down in a chair facing Peterson's cluttered desk and looked around the office: piles of reports stacked everywhere; a series of awards collecting dust on one wall; a picture of Peterson with a newborn baby.

"Jake's two now," Peterson suddenly announced. He leaked a tired smile. "I work so much, I'm not sure he even recognizes me anymore."

Kirsten frowned. In all her time dealing with the detective, she'd never once thought about his own life.

Peterson moved in front of Kirsten and sat against the edge of his desk. "So how close did this guy get to you?" he asked as he flipped open a notepad.

"Maybe half a block. Or a bit closer . . . ," Kirsten answered. "As soon as he saw the building's doorman come over, he took off."

"Sure," Peterson concluded. "Out in broad

daylight like that? Jones was taking a real risk in going after you."

Kirsten felt another shiver overtake her. "I guess he did see me the other night."

"I'll say he did," Peterson exclaimed. "You marched right into a serious drug dealer's point of operation, asking all sorts of things about him? Of course he's going to come looking for you, Kirsten."

"I had no idea what I was getting myself into," Kirsten admitted. She knew she had acted rashly the other night, but she didn't realize how far Jones would go.

"Hey, don't beat yourself up about it, Kirsten." Peterson moved toward her, placing a hand on her back. "Truth is, you did something brave."

The young detective smiled at her; Kirsten melted inside.

"Look, your placing Jones at Stop Light will make busting him much easier for us," Peterson continued. "I just don't want you—"

"Acting like a maniac," Kirsten finished his sentence and smirked. She was happy that Peterson was finally taking her seriously—and also happy to let the police take over.

Peterson smiled. "We won't let anything bad happen to you, Kirsten," he said. "You can count on it."

"Thanks again," Kirsten said to the policeman who rode in the elevator with her up to her apartment.

"No sweat, Ms. Sawyer." The cop nodded.

The elevator door opened into the foyer of the penthouse apartment.

"I *promise* to stay home tonight." Kirsten smiled, trying to put the cop at ease. "No more tracking drug-dealing killers on my own, okay?"

"Good to hear," the officer said. "Have a nice night."

Kirsten stepped out of the elevator and waved to the officer just as the elevator door closed. She tossed her purse on a nearby chair and turned toward her bedroom.

An unfamiliar feeling crept over her for the first time in a long time. A warm feeling. The muscles in her face and neck felt looser.

I feel safe! Kirsten realized. *Finally.* She felt happy. Comfortable. Although she'd come close to danger, she had also come closer to the truth. Now it seemed as if it was only a matter of time. . . .

As Kirsten approached her room, she thought about Kate's words of encouragement today. But as she faced her door, her throat tightened.

The door was slightly open, and she had *distinctly* remembered shutting it that morning—pulling it tight as she hurried off to work. Her parents weren't home, and their maid had cleaned the apartment yesterday.

Am I just overreacting? she asked herself as she slowly backed down the hallway.

CRASH!

Something fell in her room!

Someone's in there! Kirsten filled with panic, but she resisted the impulse to scream. Maybe she could slip out in time. Maybe the police officer was still double-parked outside. She hurried to the elevator, pressing the call button a million times.

But it was too late.

Someone emerged from her bedroom—letting the door slam open against the wall!

"Noooo!" Kirsten cried.

21

Brandon Yardley burst

out of Kirsten's bedroom, his eyes wild. "What did you find?" he yelled, rushing at her, his body swaying and banging into the walls of the narrow hallway.

"W-w-what are you talking about?" Kirsten stammered, backing away from the elevator—away from Brandon—and toward the kitchen. *How did he get in? I'm not even safe in my own house!*

"I followed you to Sam's house the other day!" Brandon yelled, clearly agitated and unstable. "What were you doing there?"

"Nothing!" Kirsten protested, but inside, her mind was racing. Maybe if she could make it to the kitchen, she'd be able to grab the biggest knife and scare Brandon out of there.

"I don't believe you!" Clearly Brandon wasn't into reason right about now.

"She was my best friend, Brandon! Ever think I just wanted to visit her parents?" Kirsten asked.

"How sweet!" Brandon said. "So you didn't *find* anything? Or should I say find *out* anything?"

Before Kirsten could round the corner and slip into the kitchen, Brandon reached out and grabbed her wrist.

Okay, Kirsten thought as she winced in pain. So Brandon knew that she knew. All of a sudden, Kirsten went limp. She relaxed, giving in to Brandon's tugging, even falling into his arms. *Time to switch strategies,* she thought. Instead of avoiding Brandon, she was going to use him. Brandon was going to tell her everything she needed to know . . . about Jones . . . and Sam. Everything!

"What's going on with you?" Brandon said frowning.

"Okay, you got me," Kirsten said quietly, demurely, as she looked into Brandon's saucer-size pupils. "I *did* find something at Sam's house. Something about *you.*"

Time to play, she thought.

"Tell me!" Brandon demanded.

Kirsten prayed that her plan would work.

"Why do I have to say anything?" Kirsten asked. "You know what was in those notes, Brandon. The ones you thought were so *secret.* You know, the ones where you and Sam were talking about Jones."

"The notes!" Brandon cried.

"Yup." Kirsten looked into Brandon's eyes. "And I know *all* about it. All about you and Sam and Jones! Sam told me *everything.*"

"No!" Brandon slammed his fist against a wall. "Sam promised me she'd let it all go until . . ."

"Well, it looks like she broke that promise," Kirsten replied. She was improvising everything. Buying time. Trying to get him to say more.

"I knew it!" Brandon cried. "Right before we broke up, Sam said she was going to tell everybody at Woodley. I knew that you'd be the first person she told. You guys were inseparable!"

"Of course we were," Kirsten said.

Brandon stalked into Kirsten's living room as if he had lived there his whole life.

Stay a while, Brandon, Kirsten thought. He

slumped into her father's favorite chair and ran a hand through his hair. "Look on the bright side. At least there are no more secrets." She sat on the ottoman directly across from the chair.

"I've been trying to get to you for *days*, Kirsten!" Brandon groaned.

"What do you mean?" Kirsten asked. "I haven't seen you for a while."

"Yeah," Brandon grinned. "But I saw *you*! I was here the other night, Kirsten." He let out a low, weird laugh. "In your bedroom!"

Of course! Kirsten realized. It was *Brandon* who had broken in the other night!

"You shouldn't leave a spare key under your doormat, Kirsten." Brandon smiled. "There are a lot of nut-jobs out there."

And I'm looking at one, Kirsten realized. He looked terrible. His eyes were surrounded by purplish yellow circles and his hands moved around in his lap, stuck in a constant nervous dance. She had to either get Brandon back on the topic of Jones or out of her house. "So, did everything turn out okay . . . with Jones?"

"Are you crazy?" Brandon cried. "What did Sam tell you?"

Kirsten shrugged. "A lot," she said. "Did you ever go back to Volume?"

Brandon shook his head. "No," he said. "I didn't."

"Look," Kirsten said, leaning closer to him. "I don't want to judge you, but it's kind of hard knowing only one side of the story. Now I want to hear *your* side, Brandon. It's only fair," she said. *Did it work? Is he going to tell me what I need to know?*

Brandon was quiet for a long time. Then he let out a long, weary sigh. "It was all about the drugs. You know how corny all those health classes were? Well, I guess maybe the teachers knew what they were talking about. Drugs . . . suck," he admitted.

"Tell me about it," Kirsten chimed in, encouraging Brandon to continue.

"They literally *suck*," Brandon said. "They suck your ambition. They suck your identity. Shit, they even suck your blood!"

Kirsten nodded her head, doing her best Dr. Fitzgerald impersonation.

"Anyway." Brandon cleared his throat with a shuddering hack. "Jones was my dealer, right?

"I was into coke pretty bad back then, and

I owed his people a ton of money. I tried to ask Jones for more time, 'cause my dad froze all my credit cards, but Jones wasn't having it. He *never* let anyone off the hook. He made me one of his runners as 'punishment.'"

"Right, sure," Kirsten chimed in, pretending to know the story that Brandon was beginning to unfold.

"And I have to admit, I kind of liked it. At first it was cool, you know? Being a dealer. I got to know everyone, I made a little pocket money on the side, and I got girls. *Lots* of girls." Brandon smiled for a moment, then went on. "But eventually I just got sick of it," he said. "I was sick of hiding from cops. And I was helping people snort their *lives* away, you know? Kids!

"When I tried to get out of the game, Jones told me that he'd expose me. He'd tell my parents! He'd get me kicked off the JV basketball team at Talcott!"

"I remember hearing about that," Kirsten lied.

"Yeah!" Brandon yelled. He was worked up now. "At first I did what Jones said, and kept dealing, but then one day I said, 'Screw it!' I told my parents all about my problem and my dealing. They notified the police about Jones, and he was arrested. Luckily, my dad hushed things up at Talcott, seeing how everyone was studying in the *Yardley Library*, after all!" He grinned.

And so did Kirsten. The story was becoming clearer.

"I had to leave the school, but my record was *spotless*. That's when I started going to Woodley—and by senior year, I was dating Sam. I wasn't dealing anymore, but I was still doing a ton of blow. Sammy even got into it for a while."

How could I not know that Sam was into coke? Kirsten wondered, but she quickly corrected herself. Sam had given her a hit of E that night at the Party Room. Sam had been more of a partier than Kirsten ever knew. She nodded her head as if she'd heard it all before.

"But when she saw how crazy it made me," Brandon continued, "she dumped my ass. I was heated, but honestly, it was a smart move for her. I was a mess. I guess I still am."

Brandon looked up at Kirsten and made an attempt at an apologetic smile. In that moment, he looked so vulnerable. So weak. Inside that big, tough body was just a little boy.

"And you know the rest . . ." Brandon trailed off.

"Wait!" Kirsten heard herself shout. She held her tongue. If she sounded too eager, Brandon would realize that she didn't know a thing.

"I know *Sam's* version, but it didn't make *you* look so good," she said. "What do you have to defend yourself for, Brandon?" Kirsten asked.

Brandon squinted at Kirsten. He seemed suspicious.

"I just want to know," Kirsten added.

Brandon nodded. "I know, I know," he said. "When Jones got out of jail, he tracked me down and said that I owed him money. He gave me just one week to pay them off. Or else they'd KILL ME! Even though Sam and I were over by then, she felt bad for me and tried to pay off Jones. And that's why she was seeing him. That's why she was with him that night in the Party Room."

At last, Kirsten thought. *The mystery is coming together!*

Kirsten tried to conceal the wide smile spreading across her face. She had something! Something concrete that could help her find the real murderer—Jones!

"But she never came home that night, so Jones is still out there . . . and he's looking for me," Brandon said as he slumped further into the chair. "I know it."

"You don't have to worry anymore, Brandon." Kirsten reached out to him. He seemed so scared now. "I've told the cops about Jones already."

"You what?" Brandon suddenly jumped out of the chair. The color drained from his face.

"I told them to arrest Jones." Kirsten furrowed her brow "We'll finally learn what happened to Sam. And once he's in jail, you'll be off the hook."

"No!" Brandon yelled. "They'll never catch him. And when Jones finds out that someone turned him in again, who do you think he'll go after first?" Brandon cursed over and over, slamming his fist into his open palm. "I'm a dead man!" he cried.

22

"A dead man!" Brandon cried again. His gaze darted around the room as if he wasn't sure what to do next. Then he tore out of there and into the elevator.

"Brandon, wait!" Kirsten said, but it was no use. The elevator doors closed.

Minutes later she could see him from her living room window, racing out of the building and flagging down a cab.

Oh, my God, she thought. She had played Brandon perfectly, but had she also sentenced him to death?

And Jones was still out there. Somewhere.

Oh, Sam, Kirsten thought. *Why did you get involved in all of this? Maybe if you had stayed away from Brandon and Jones, you wouldn't have died. Or maybe if you had told me that you were in trouble, I could have helped. Maybe you'd still be alive today.*

But now Kirsten had someone else to worry about: Brandon.

When does this story end? Kirsten wondered. *When does a new one begin?*

She walked groggily into her bathroom and splashed water onto her face. It was late already. Time to crash. *For a week.*

Kirsten looked at her reflection in the mirror and inspected the lines across her forehead, the glazed look in her eyes. She looked like a thirty-year-old even though she still wasn't old enough to buy her own smokes.

Whatever, she thought, walking into her bedroom and changing into a pair of silk pajamas. She crossed to the window, pushed it open, and sat carefully on the ledge. She hugged her knees as she stared down at what looked like a sea of yellow cabs and wondered if Brandon had made it home all right.

Kirsten craned her head slightly out of the window and took in a deep breath. *I guess it's time to go to bed,* she thought. As Kirsten stepped back inside her room, something down on the street caught her eye. She noticed someone standing in the middle of the street, wearing a baseball cap and sunglasses.

Sunglasses at night? Kirsten thought. *Why?*

From her vantage point it almost looked as if the guy was staring back at her. In this gigantic city, two random people could still cross sightlines from such a great distance.

Wait! Maybe it isn't random!

The figure across the street waved.

To who? To me? Kirsten wondered. Unsure of what she was seeing, Kirsten blinked her eyes. When the stranger took off his sunglasses, however, all doubt vanished. Kirsten immediately recognized the figure from twelve stories up:

It was Kyle!

Without thinking, Kirsten threw on something and hurried downstairs. Now that the truth was out there, she had so much to tell Kyle! She couldn't wait!

After a quick elevator ride, Kirsten hurried out onto the street, looking everywhere for Kyle. It was colder than she'd expected. She shivered in her simple white T-shirt and shorts as she approached the corner, expecting to see Kyle waiting for her.

She turned the corner and looked for him everywhere, but he was gone.

Fear crept back into her mind. Maybe it

wasn't such a bright idea to go running out into the middle of the night for a wanted man.

Just as Kirsten started to leave, confused and worried, Kyle stepped out from the shadows. She softened when she saw him smile. Then, without thinking, she reached out and hugged him. Grabbing Kyle hard, holding on as if her life depended on it, Kirsten whispered, "I thought I'd never see you again."

Kyle, surprised by the hug, stepped back a little. "I didn't think you wanted to see me." He frowned. "I didn't know whether you believed me."

"I was afraid, Kyle," she confessed. "You'd lied to me before. You were wanted by the police."

"So why'd you come down this time, then?" he pressed.

"Because I know something." Kirsten smiled.

Kyle's face brightened ever so slightly. "Tell me. . . ."

"The red-haired guy—that guy who left with Sam that night—"

"Uh-huh." Kyle was hanging on to her every word.

"He was extorting Brandon, and when Brandon tried to put an end to it. Sam tried to help him and—"

"He put an end to her," Kyle finished her sentence.

"Exactly!" Kirsten cried. At least Kyle had some kind of lead now. Something that might clear the name Paul Stone forever.

"Shh, Kirsten," Kyle reminded her, glancing around to check the street. The new evidence might clear his name, but until then, he was still a wanted man.

Just then, a police officer turned the corner. Kyle suddenly pulled Kirsten in close. Then he leaned in and kissed her to avoid being detected.

Kirsten relaxed into Kyle's soft lips as her mind swirled and her heart pounded in her chest. She had nearly forgotten how Kyle's kisses felt. And her long embrace with him felt like a welcome excuse to forget everything except being close.

So much so that Kirsten was disappointed when the cop finally shuffled across Eighty-fifth Street. She pulled away from Kyle to catch her breath and stop a spark from quickly turning into a fire.

"Maybe after all this—" Kyle began awkwardly, looking down at his feet.

"Maybe," Kirsten cut him off. "But not yet, Kyle. Not now."

"Okay." He looked at her with calm, understanding eyes.

A siren started up down the block, and Kyle jumped. He glanced over his shoulder for a moment and then slipped a folded piece of paper into Kirsten's hand. "Here, take this. . . . I'm hiding at The Lisbon." He leaned in quickly, this time giving her a sweet kiss on the cheek. "I'll be in touch," he whispered and, with that, he disappeared back into the shadows.

Romance can wait, Kirsten thought. *But how long will it take before the nightmare is over?*

As she walked back into her building, thinking about *that kiss,* her cell phone rang. She pulled the phone out from her pocked and stared at the caller I.D., which said, UNKNOWN NUMBER.

Who's this? she wondered, and answered the phone.

It was Peterson.

He never sleeps! Kirsten thought.

"Good news. We have Jones in custody," he said.

"Oh, my God!" Kirsten screamed. She was blown away. "I'll come down to identify him!"

"No need." Peterson laughed. "We got enough drug charges on this goon to keep him off the streets for a *while*, Kirsten. That'll be enough time to investigate Sam Byrne's and Emma Harris's murders."

"Yes!" Kirsten wanted to reach right through that phone line and hug the detective.

"And you'd better *believe* that Jones isn't posting bail. That's how he gave us the slip last time!"

Peterson went on—something about trial dates for Sam's case—but Kirsten couldn't hear anymore. She broke into a flood of tears.

"Thank you!" she sobbed into the phone line as Peterson went on. "Thank you!"

Finally the past could stay in the past.

Finally it was over.

Part Three

23

"*Love Stinks!*" Kirsten

Sawyer cheered from the tech room at WXRJ. It was the day after the police had arrested Jones, and Kirsten was brimming with new energy. Now that Sam's and Emma's killer was behind bars, she could get back to her work in a serious way. "How may I help you?" she asked a caller on the phone.

"I was hoping to talk to Kate," a distressed voice answered back.

"Absolutely. That's why we're here, sir. I'll just need a name and the nature of your call," Kirsten said, switching his line into the studio.

"Kevin," the caller said, seeming to relax a little. Then he told her that he wanted to ask Kate if it was possible to love your kitty *too* much.

"All right, Kevin, I'm going to transfer your call, and the next voice will be Dr. Grisholm's. . . ."

Swiveling around in her chair, Kirsten entered "crazy for kitty" into the computer and smiled as she breezed through her job like an old pro. *This is how work should go every day,* she thought. Now that she was off the pills and the killer was off the streets, she could behave like an actual human being.

Kate smiled at her and took the call.

Kirsten leaned back in her chair and pictured Kyle standing outside her building again. She closed her eyes and imagined their kiss. Now she had even better news to tell him. Yesterday he had given her a sweet letter that included his cell phone number and address. But this was something that she wanted to tell him in person. *I'll go to The Lisbon as soon as I can,* she decided.

As Kirsten thought about the *next* kiss she and Kyle would share, she spotted Brian entering the tech room with his head down. "Hey there, surfer boy." But before Kirsten could even finish her sentence, Brian grabbed a microphone stand and darted back out.

Kirsten ran into the hallway only to watch Brian hurry away. Even though his hickeys were fading, his ears were bright red.

She laughed out loud. He had been avoiding Kirsten all day, ducking her at the water cooler, pretending to be reading a magazine in the mailroom. He had even faced the back of the elevator on the ride up to work!

Kirsten was blown away by Brian's transformation: He had come to New York pretty naive, but Leslie Fenk had turned him quickly to the dark side. And her little surfer boy seemed a little embarrassed about it.

As Kirsten shook her head and walked back into the tech room, her cell phone rang the song "Rock Your Body."

It was Julie's cheesy Justin Timberlake ring! The girls had programmed the same ring into each of their phones so they'd know when the other was calling. Kirsten was dying to talk to Julie, but suddenly she felt nervous. *What do I say?* she wondered. *How can I patch things up?*

Kirsten flipped her phone open anxiously, careful to move out of her boss's line of sight. "Hello, Julie?"

"Hey," Julie replied softly, sounding still bruised from their fight.

There was a long pause. An eternity. Finally, Kirsten decided to clear the air: "Julie, I am soooo sorry. I never meant to—"

"Kenny Dwiggler was a hottie!" Julie broke in with her shrillest voice and familiar laugh.

"Yeah! A total hottie!" Kirsten played along. "And I'm a total bitch," she added more seriously.

"The biggest in all Manhattan?" Julie asked.

"Now don't get carried away, slut!" Kirsten laughed.

It felt good to joke around with her friend again. In fact, it felt amazing. Kirsten leaned back in her chair and smiled. "So when do I get to see your beautiful face?" she asked. She couldn't wait to see her best friend. They had so much to talk about.

"Tonight?" Julie smacked gum on the other line.

"Just tell me where and I'm there," Kirsten said.

"Duh!" Julie cried. "The Party Room!"

* * *

Three hours and twenty-seven minutes later, Kirsten and Julie were once again attached at the hip, gossiping on the back couches at their favorite bar.

"'Dear Kiiirrsssten,'" Julie *ooh-la-la*-ed as she began reading Kyle's note to Kirsten—the one he had slipped her on the street.

"Just read the damn note, Jules!" Kirsten laughed. She was so happy to be hanging out with Julie at the Party Room again. Just like old times. She had just finished telling Julie all about Jones and her latest meeting with Kyle. Now she was excited to share Kyle's sweeter side. . . .

"'In the blur of the past few months,'" Julie read on, "'I've never stopped thinking about you. I'm sorry I brought you into all this, Kirsten, but I'm not sorry that I fell for you.'" Julie looked up from the note and squeezed Kirsten's arm. "And the panties are off!"

"Slow down, Pembroke. I'm a good girl." Kirsten winked.

"But why's he staying at The Lisbon?" Julie asked, reading the address Kyle had scribbled on the bottom of the note. "It's such a dump."

"Really?" Kirsten was surprised. Kyle had plenty of money.

"It's right near my yoga class in Midtown," Julie added. "I think you can actually pay for your room with crystal."

"I guess the crappier the place, the easier it is to hide," Kirsten suggested. She took the note back from Julie and folded it into her purse.

"Whatever you say, daaahling," Julie drawled in her old, overly done rich-bitch voice.

She was back. Julie was back! Kirsten suddenly sprang forward and hugged her friend.

Julie let out a fake "oof!" and squeezed her right back.

The two friends shared a long, much-needed hug until Scott came by, festive as ever, balancing two gorgeous drinks on a round cork tray. "Pomegranate Martinis for the VIPs in the back," he said.

"Now we're talking!" Julie shouted.

Scott passed Kirsten her drink, but she put up her hand. "No thanks, sweetie. I'm taking a break from the booze for a while. Just Diet Cokes and Pellegrino for me for now."

"Whoa!" Scott looked a little surprised, then said, "Your wish is my command."

Kirsten winked at Scott. "Thanks, genie."

"So you're not drinking with me?" Julie asked as Scott left to get Kirsten a kinder and gentler drink. Julie picked up the two martinis. She tilted her head and frowned as she stared at the drinks, then at Kirsten. "You sure?"

Kirsten nodded. She hoped that this wasn't going to be a problem for Julie, because they were older—almost in college—and she didn't want to have to deal with the whole peer-pressure thing.

But then Julie broke into a giggle and took two large sips from each martini. "That just means more for me!"

Kirsten laughed as her friend went to town on the drinks.

Julie put the martinis down and grabbed Kirsten's hands. "I'm proud of you. You look great. You've really pulled yourself together, girl."

"Yeah, Kirsten," Scott agreed as he bussed empty glasses from the surrounding tables. "Sometimes you have to back away from all this craziness and find your limits."

"Thanks, guys," Kirsten said sweetly. It meant a lot to her to have her friends' support.

"But just 'cause you're on the wagon doesn't mean you can't party!" Julie smiled as she pulled a flyer out of her purse.

Kirsten looked down at a glossy photo of the Brooklyn Bridge with the word BROOKNASTY stamped in bright yellow across the bottom. "What's this?" she asked.

"Oh, I don't know . . . ," Julie said, "only the biggest dance party of the entire year! It's in Brooklyn. Right on the water. Tomorrow night!"

"Oh yeah, Brooknasty," Scott chimed in. "Big bash. Very cool. Too bad I'll be working!" he said as he hurried back over to the bar.

Julie watched Scott walk away for a moment, licked her lips, and then spun back to face Kirsten again. "Listen, Kirsten: Everyone we now know, ever *knew*, or ever dreamed about knowing is bound to be there," she continued, pinching Kirsten's side. "It's must-see TV!"

"Well then, we're there, baby!" Kirsten grinned as visions of fabulous outfits danced in her head. Why not? Detective Peterson had Jones, and soon Kyle's name would be cleared. It was definitely time to celebrate, right?

24

I love it!

I really do!

I really, really love it!

*IREALLYFUCKINGLOVEHOWGODDAMN-
STUPIDYOUCOULDBE!*

*Thought they had me for a second, but they
don't! They NEVER WILL!*

*Calm down. Control. Keep cool. Refrigerate
after opening . . .*

I'm not going to lose it now.

Do you think I'm crazy or something?

But here, my friend, here is my final question:

Do you really think it's that easy?

*You actually think this story wraps up like
some nice little present sitting under a Christmas
tree?*

Think again.

*I just need to change direction. And watch my
back.*

Just need to think. And find some fresh air. Breathe a little.

Then ATTACK!

I'll finally settle this thing once and for all.

But that's the problem with all of you. You don't want the truth. It's too ugly. Too complex. You want everything so damn simple and happy and right.

But I've got news for you: There's a lot that's wrong. A lot I gotta make right.

You might think the story is over—but trust me, it's not.

It hasn't even started!

25

THUMP, THUMP, THUMP!

Bass reverberated through the moving bodies. A jazz trumpet rose above the sweaty dance floor, mingling with the wide Manhattan skyline.

It was Saturday night in Brooklyn, and the party was hot! Ridiculous.

A live house-music band played furiously, with the Chrysler Building as a backdrop and some five hundred pulsing people as the foreground.

Brooknasty is right! Kirsten thought as she let go of Julie's hand. She laughed and threw her head back, watching stars dance in the hazy sky above.

The party took place in a large, roofless warehouse, surrounded by high metal walls. Kirsten felt as if she were in some postmodern coliseum. The spectacle of the day didn't have to do with fighting or lions, though, just raw beats and sex.

The music rolled through Kirsten's entire body as she slid from person to person. She released all her inhibitions and spun around. Julie was now a few yards away, dancing with some college guy, and also having the time of her life.

Although Kirsten was getting farther and farther away from her friend, she didn't fight the movement of the crowd. The band switched to a salsa number—something fast and furious. Kirsten found herself being swept up by a Latino hottie who wore an old guayabera and gave her a wide, disarming smile.

Why not? Kirsten decided in an instant, letting him spin her around and around. They snapped into a solid salsa stance, and he led her through a dance routine that cleared the floor around them.

Thank you, dance class, Kirsten thought as she kept up remarkably well. When he placed a hand behind her back, she grabbed for it. With dexterity and grace, he whipped her through a long, winding move. The crowd cheered for them.

"Alejandro," he said politely as he dipped Kirsten at the end of the song. He thanked her "for the pleasure" and walked away.

Kirsten smiled at the fun-loving partyers around her and then looked up for Julie, but all she saw was an ocean of dancers. She headed toward the bar to find her friend, slithering her way though the swaying, grinding bodies on the dance floor.

And speaking of grinding, Kirsten ran directly into Leslie and Brian. Leslie was running her hands up the front of Brian's shirt, kissing him sloppily on the neck and face. *No shame in their game.* Kirsten laughed to herself, happy that she had never hooked up with Brian. She tried to avoid them, but Leslie noticed her out of the corner of her eye.

"Kirstennnn!" Leslie called. Her eyes were as wide as saucers, and her pupils were dilated. Clearly the girl was gone on something. "I want you to meet Byronnnnn. My new boyyyfriennnd!"

Was Leslie for real? Was she *that* bad a friend? Was she *that* big a bitch?

Brian looked up, eyes smoked-out, mouth pasty from dehydration. He had on a strategically ripped Diesel T-Shirt and a Von-Dutch trucker hat. "Already know her," he mumbled, turning back to tongue Leslie some more.

Kirsten just shook her head and kept dancing toward the bar. She thought about Brian's metamorphosis—from nice to nasty. He was a completely different person all in a matter of weeks.

As Kirsten scanned the party for Julie again, she noticed an elevated section near the back. *Must be the VIP section,* she realized as she saw hipsters juggling bottles of Cristal, bouncers checking I.D.s, supermodels, deejays, and some rock-star wannabe with red hair—

Wait! Kirsten gasped. How many guys had hair like that? Air escaped her lungs faster than she could breathe it back in. She stumbled back, reaching out to the people around her to steady herself. There, standing in the middle of the VIP section, was a guy with red hair and sunglasses. It couldn't be, but . . .

JONES!

How? Kirsten's mind reeled. *He's supposed to be in jail! No bail. That's what Peterson said.*

This wasn't fair! Just as Kirsten's world was

building back up, it came crumbling right back down again! Why was he out of jail?

Kirsten instinctively ducked into the crowd and made her way toward the ladies' room. Someone in the crowd elbowed her accidentally, and Kirsten crashed into someone's drink.

Beer and sweat all mixed together in one long smear down the front of Kirsten's dress. Not caring about how she looked, however, she pushed the rest of the way to the bathroom. Her heart pounded as she cut the long line of women waiting outside the bathroom and she slid into a stall.

"Bitch!" a chorus of women rang out, but Kirsten didn't care.

Jones was out there. Free, somehow.

She wanted *out* of Brooknasty—and she wanted it now!

Where the hell is Julie? she wondered.

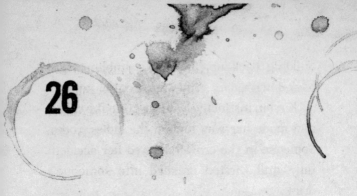

26

Where the hell is Kirsten?
Julie wondered as she pulled herself out from between two moshing frat boys. "Ever heard of 'excuse me'!" she yelled at them. *I am so over this place.*

The last time she saw Kirsten, she was dancing with some Latin cutie. Julie had gone to the bar for a drink, and when she'd turned around, Kirsten was nowhere to be found. Now the scene was changing, and the crowded dance floor was turning aggressive, almost hostile.

"Ugghh!" Julie yelled as someone flung a soaked T-shirt in her face. *Brooknasty is just straight-up nasty!* she decided as she wiped sweat from her hair. *And where the hell is Kirsten!* she wondered again.

"Kirsten!" she shouted out, but she couldn't compete with that jangling guitar line blaring over the speakers. *I just want to go home already,* she thought. *This is too much.*

And to make matters worse, Julie couldn't find Kirsten anywhere. They hadn't been separated for that long, but in place like this, time was relative.

A tall, skinny guy rushed up to Julie and grabbed her by the waist. "Dance with me, baby!" He stared into her eyes. His breath smelled like sewage, and he looked like a zombie—an extra from *Evil Dead II.*

"No thanks!" Julie yelled as she pushed him off and continued toward the VIP section. At least there she could wait in style. But as the music picked up tempo, Julie suddenly felt the urge to go outside—*really* outside. Even though she could see the sky above, she felt too . . . boxed in.

Gotta get some air, she said to herself, but she didn't want to leave the party alone. "Kirsten!" she yelled one final time.

Now she was *really* starting to feel claustrophobic. A hot tingle overtook her face, and each of her breaths became labored, uneven. Ever since the time when she was four and had got stuck in a Barneys elevator for six hours, close spaces hadn't quite agreed with her.

Julie found her bright pink cell phone and tried Kirsten's number. The problem was, however, that she couldn't even hear her *own* phone ringing. As music blasted, she strained to listen to the call.

Nothing.

Lost at sea, Julie joked to herself as she looked across the massive dance party. Finally resolved to so *something*, Julie took a deep breath and plowed her way to the bar. She knocked into a stand of anorexic Brearley girls without saying a word to them. She'd make it up on the tennis courts.

Plus, Julie didn't have time to be social right now. She was starting to feel strange. Her stomach sloshed with acid, and she felt a burning in her throat. She wondered if the three hot dogs she'd wolfed down at Gray's Papaya earlier had anything to do with it. No matter how rich her family was, Julie swore she'd never stop eating those skinny, salty dogs.

That is, until tonight.

As Julie felt the sickness surging in her stomach, she spotted a velvet curtain leading somewhere. *Anywhere is better than here,* she thought as she made her way to the dark red exit.

Finally reaching the high metal wall, Julie pushed through the curtain and stumbled out into an alley.

Outside. Ahhh. After taking a huge, greedy breath of air, Julie opened her eyes and looked around: She was standing alone at the edge of an abandoned, bottle-strewn lot.

SLAM!

Julie felt her heart drop to the concrete as she spun back around. A large door banged closed in front of the velvet curtain she had just exited.

Where did that door come from? she wondered. The soft velvet entrance was now barred with a thick metal door. *Weird.* Julie scrunched up her face in confusion. She rushed back to the door and pulled on the handle, but it wouldn't open.

What? Julie suddenly panicked. The door wasn't budging, and she was trapped on the wrong side.

"Hello!" she screamed, half annoyed, half scared. She banged on the metal door with all her might, but no one came to open it. *They probably can't hear me!* she thought, banging again and again and again until her hands started to ache.

Julie frowned and rubbed her hand. The night was going from bad to worse. "And I looked so cute tonight," she said out loud, glancing down at her poofy Carrie Bradshaw skirt. Now, it looked more like a dead lily. "What a waste."

Julie hugged herself and breathed into her hands. She was wearing practically nothing, and it was starting to get chilly out there. "Hello!" she shouted to no one in particular. She listened to her voice echo across the abandoned lot. A new, more intense shiver washed over her as she suddenly felt vulnerable. She was all alone.

Stop being such a wuss, Julie scolded herself, but she couldn't help it. She didn't like the creepy quietness. She gazed around and spotted a small shack sitting at the far end of the lot. A dim light flickered inside. *Hel-lo . . .* There was hope. Finally.

Left with no alternative, Julie started off toward the structure, stepping over rusted nails, bicycle tires, beer cans, and shattered fifths of Thunderbird. She hoped there was someone inside the shack—a security guard or something—someone who could help her get back inside the party so she could find Kirsten.

"Hello?" Julie's voice squeaked as she neared the building.

No answer.

She peeked inside the shack through a dirty window and spotted a lone red candle dripping on the center of the floor, but no one was inside.

Weird, she thought, getting the sudden feeling that maybe coming out there hadn't been such a bright idea. She backed away from the house.

Then someone rushed her from behind. "Arrrrrrhhhhhhhh!" he yelled as he knocked her to the ground, facefirst.

"No!" Julie screamed, suddenly recalling all the self-defense classes she had taken at the 92nd Street Y. She moved to kick her attacker, but failed as she got caught up in something.

Oh, my God! Julie realized. He was wrapping her around and around in a red cloth.

Then dragging her . . . dragging her into the shed.

"Let me go!" Julie screamed again, and tried to claw her way out of the cotton web, but there was no escape.

As a hood pulled tightly over her head, the last thing Julie saw was a red-haired man. . . .

27

"Julie!" Kirsten yelled

again, her voice hoarse. *Where are you?* she wondered. Despair was beginning to set in. Even though it was already one in the morning, the party was just building up momentum. The crowd had multiplied so much, there was no room to move *anywhere* anymore, let alone find someone. Club kids filled the dance floor with shrill whistles and bouncing neon necklaces. The band had been replaced by a bald female deejay. She was spinning techno music and bopping her body to a rambunctious beat.

It was on.

The party roared like a growling beast.

And somewhere out there, Jones was lurking.

Kirsten trembled now. All the fear that had seemingly dissipated over that last couple of days came rushing back into her body. She hoped that Julie was just off being her usual self, making out with some guy in a dark corner somewhere—and not in trouble.

Kirsten *prayed* that this was the case.

After a serious struggle, Kirsten made it to a far corner of the party and stepped outside through a thick velvet curtain. Feeling the coolness of outside air, she found herself standing in a dark, empty lot.

Finally able to hear herself think, Kirsten dialed Julie's phone again.

Still no answer.

Kirsten's arm dropped to the side. She let her phone ring for a while, waiting for Julie's voice mail to activate. *Useless,* she thought, but just as she turned to go back inside, she heard something. Or at least *thought* she heard something.

Kirsten stood still and listened intently. Faintly in the distance she could make out . . . "Rock Your Body."

It was Julie's Justin Timberlake ring.

Filled with another gust of energy, Kirsten spun around to see where the ringing was coming from. Across the large abandoned lot, she saw a dark metal shack of some kind. It seemed as if the sound was coming from that direction!

Why are you out there, *Julie?* Kirsten wanted to ask. *And why aren't you picking up your goddamn phone?!*

Kirsten's mind burned, and she started out across the lot, trampling through the refuse. As she neared the shack, her heart practically imploded when she heard a muffled cry for help coming from inside.

Julie's in trouble! Kirsten was sure of it. She ran faster and faster toward the door. Her shoes fell off, but she kept running, right into the metal siding, breaking down the door and tumbling inside.

That's when she saw Julie, tied up in a chair, eyes wide with fear! "Julie!" Kirsten hurried to free her friend from the cocoon of tattered red cloth. A stream of blood ran from Julie's nose into her shirt collar, collecting in a dark, shimmering puddle. Her face was scratched as well, and a jagged cloth stretched from one swollen cheek to the other.

Kirsten ripped the gag out of Julie's mouth.

"Red-haired guy!" Julie's voice was garbled with panic and blood. "Grabbed me!"

Kirsten held Julie's hands tightly and

stared directly into her eyes. Wild, flitting eyes. "Where is he?" she asked Julie. She needed her help now. *Both* of their lives depended on it. Jones could be anywhere. She shot a quick glance toward the door, then turned back to Julie. "Where is he?"

"Gone," Julie finally gasped. Then she looked down, taken over by racking sobs.

"What is it, Julie?" Kirsten begged. "Are you okay? You can tell me."

"He told me he'd KILL ME, Kirsten!" Julie sucked in short breaths between sobs. "If I didn't—"

But then, Julie's voice cut off. She hung her head as if she was defeated.

"If you didn't *what*, Julie?" Kirsten asked, her heart pounding with adrenaline.

"If I didn't tell him where Kyle was hiding!" Julie broke into a fit of sobs again. "So I did!"

Kirsten could feel her heart sliding away, melting into acid in her chest. They had to get to Kyle—fast! She finished untying Julie and practically dragged her out of the chair. Out of the shack.

Faster! Faster! her mind screamed as she began running. She tugged on Julie's arm to help her keep pace. Kirsten then reached into her purse, pulled out her cell phone, and speed-dialed Kyle with her free hand.

Got to warn him! she repeated over and over in her mind, numb to the glass and metal that poked and cut her bare feet.

Kirsten strained to listen to her phone. After a series of crackles and stalls, she barely made out a voice. "Kyle, is that you?" she cried out desperately.

She stopped to listen, letting her terrified best friend catch her breath for a minute. Julie moaned now, her legs buckling under the stress of what she had just been through.

The phone connection was awful. And there was only one power bar left on Kirsten's phone.

"Kyle! Can you hear me?"

And then, finally, the best sound Kirsten had ever heard in her seventeen years on the planet came over the line: a garbled "Yes."

"Run, Kyle! Get out of there. Just leave. Right now! Get the hell out of The Lisbon!" she cried.

More static.

Julie was leaning against her now, pulling Kirsten down.

"Kyle! Did you hear what I said?" she screamed into the phone. "Go!"

" . . . figured it out!" Kirsten heard just the smallest fragment of what Kyle was saying.

Had he heard her at all?

" . . . know who the murderer is . . ."

Before Kirsten could ask any questions, the line went dead.

She speed-dialed again, but her battery failed.

In a moment of sheer rage, Kirsten chucked her phone across the street. Then she snapped back to life and physically carried Julie the rest of the way across the lot. She found a small, but workable tear in the large chain-link fence surrounding the property.

"Hello! Help!" Kirsten yelled out for her car-service driver as she guided Julie through the jagged opening.

Julie moaned again as she sprawled out across the sidewalk on the other side.

"Julie!" Kirsten cried. She had to get her home. She scraped through the rusty opening herself, grabbing high above her head to stabilize herself.

She felt something strange—something soft and silky—and she looked up:

There, hooked right to the fence, was a wig. It was the exact color of Jones's hair.

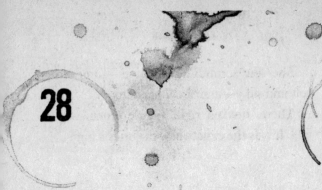

28

"**Pick up, pick up, pick** *up . . . ,*" Kirsten murmured as she called Kyle for what seemed like the hundredth time on Julie's cell phone. But he didn't pick up, and the phone rang and rang as the black Lincoln ripped uptown, skidding over potholes, revving across intersections toward The Lisbon.

Kirsten's driver would drop her off first and had agreed to make sure that Julie made it safely into her East Eighty-fourth Street townhouse.

Kirsten hung up the phone and pressed redial.

Still no answer.

Her mind reeled as she squirmed in her seat and glanced at Julie. *Who did this to you?* she asked silently. Then she envisioned that hideous red wig, hanging from the chain-link fence in Brooklyn. *And what was the deal with the wig? And what would he want with Kyle? Has he confused him with Brandon?*

Kirsten didn't know. All she knew was that she had to find him—or at least make sure that he got away.

Finally, the car skidded across Forty-second Street and slammed to a halt right outside The Lisbon. Kirsten shoved a hundred-dollar bill into Julie's palm and raced into the lobby of the hotel.

It was totally empty. Quiet, except for Musak playing in some far-off room.

"Hello!" Kirsten shouted, looking around frantically for a desk clerk. She didn't know what room Kyle was staying in.

Kirsten yelled out again. She didn't have time to waste! But her words rang through the dingy waiting room. The Lisbon *was* a dump. Sweaty wallpaper peeled onto shabby plastic couches. A cracked-out tenant mumbled to himself under a "choking victim" poster.

"What?" a voice finally cracked, and Kirsten spun around. A small Asian woman had materialized from behind the front desk. She frowned at Kirsten.

"I'm looking for someone who is staying here!" Kirsten said.

"Congratulations," the woman drawled, unmoved by Kirsten's urgency.

"He's around my age. Dark hair? Hazel eyes?"

The woman didn't budge.

"I don't know . . ." Kirsten tried to focus, but she was losing it. "He might be registered as Kyle or Paul Stone. . . ."

The woman's face was still blank.

"He's been staying here for a few nights now? He's . . . very quiet," Kirsten added.

"Maybe I know this kid," the woman finally muttered, slowly nodding her head.

"Well, can you *please* tell me which room he's in?" Kirsten pleaded. She was desperate. "It's a matter of life or death!"

"Sure, but I'm very old. Memory's not too good." The woman smirked.

Kirsten threw her final twenty at the woman. There was no time for bartering.

"10A!" the Asian woman said.

Kirsten flew into the elevator and jabbed at a worn-out button. *10A, 10A, 10A,* she chanted to herself as the elevator crept to life.

She could hear the metal cords winding as it slowly pulled upward.

Come on! Kirsten thought as the doors opened on the seventh floor.

"Going down?" an elderly man in Bermuda shorts and black socks said, smiling a toothy grin.

"NO!" Kirsten cried. She didn't have time to be nice. She pushed the tenth-floor button again, and the doors closed. When the elevator door opened just a crack on the tenth floor, Kirsten instantly slid out and ran down the hallway.

10A, 10A, 10A! Kirsten squinted in the dingy light as she checked each door. Finally she spotted Kyle's room at the very end of the hall, and broke into a run.

She noticed that Kyle's door was slightly open. *This is not good!* she thought.

She felt her body slowing down. Everything became eerily quiet. And although Kirsten was *dying* to walk through that door, she couldn't bear to do it.

Why is his door open? She felt a shiver spread up into her spine. But inside the pit of her stomach, she knew the answer. She knew. . . .

And when she pushed the door to room 10A open wide, her worst fears were confirmed. "Kyle!" she screamed, running to the limp body sprawled in the center of the room.

A pool of blood had matted his wavy brown hair and soaked a large, neat oval into the dirty tan carpeting. His eyes were open, staring . . . still staring at some unknown horror that Kirsten did not want to imagine.

Then she saw the gun.

It was on the carpet, next to his right hand.

"Noooo!" she cried out, pulling the gun from his hand. She bent over his body and pressed her ear close to his bloody mouth. His body was still warm. *Maybe he's still alive. Maybe he's breathing!*

But he wasn't. Kyle was dead.

Dead!

Kirsten had tried to warn him, but she was too late! Why? Why was this happening? Why did the people she loved keep dying?

I can't do it. I can't go through the pain again! she thought, hugging Kyle's body. She squeezed her eyes shut as tears streamed down her cheeks. *No, no, no, no!*

A few minutes later she opened her eyes

and pulled away from him. Something strange caught her eye. It was Kyle's left hand . . . balled into a fist? Why?

She leaned over him and realized that he was holding something! Gently, she pried open his hand, and a crumpled photo fell onto the floor. She picked it up and studied it.

It was picture of Kyle . . . a little younger, about seventeen or eighteen . . . and there was a girl in his arms . . . petite . . . beautiful blond hair . . .

Is this Carolee? Is this what she looked like? Kirsten wondered. *But why is he holding this?* She couldn't figure it out right then, but she knew that she'd have plenty of time—the rest of her life, maybe. She slipped the photo into her pocket.

Right now I have to call the police, Kirsten thought, standing up and glancing at the gun still in her hand. *I have to report a murder.*

"NYPD!" a uniformed officer yelled as he and four others rushed into the room—shoulder to shoulder, guns drawn.

Kirsten gasped. *Talk about perfect timing!*

She relaxed when Detective Peterson followed the initial push-through. "Detective!"

she cried, crossing the room. "Thank God! I'm so glad to—"

"Drop it, Kirsten!" Peterson said, quickly drawing his gun and pointing it at her.

Kirsten glanced at the gun in her hand. "This? No, you don't underst—"

"He said drop it!" a uniformed officer said as they all surrounded her.

Kirsten gulped and did as she was told. Her mind swirled as the detective locked her wrists into a pair of handcuffs and arrested her for the murder of Paul Stone.

THE PARTY'S ALMOST OVER!

Don't miss the thrilling conclusion of the Party Room trilogy: *Last Call*, by Morgan Burke.

She moved on to another set of familiar faces. Talcott kids she vaguely recognized who'd long since graduated—a group of friends and a kid with thick brown hair who could only be . . .

Kirsten squinted. Kyle! Back before he'd gone to jail. Back when he was a student at Talcott.

Was Jan so obsessed with the murder case? Fixated with the thing that had torn her own life apart? Some wackos collected famous people's shoes—did Jan have a Preppy Murders fetish? That had to be what this was all about. And the fact that she was rooming with him made her ill.

Kirsten backed away from the wall. A top-sheet from one of the accordion folders had stuck to her elbow, and she pulled it off: ADAMS MURDER, it said.

She turned the folder open-side up and

skimmed through the yellow legal sheets with handwritten notes, more newspaper clippings, and photos—all related to Carolee's murder. She glanced at the labels on the other folders: BYRNE MURDER, HARRIS MURDER, AUTOPSY PHOTOS. Sick.

Kirsten lifted the last folder. Swallowing hard, she looked at the top photo.

It was Sam.

Sam. Naked and ghostly pale, her eyes open as if daring the photographer to shoot, a blue bruise over one side of her face and her soft beautiful auburn hair matted by blood.

It was Sam. Dead.

Kirsten let out a gasp and dropped the folder, let it fall on the counter, spilling out more images of her best friend, side, front, close-up, full-body. And the obvious questions—How did he get these? and Why does he have them? and Who the hell is this freak?—were lost in the jangled sparks that were short-circuiting her brain.

As she backed out of the room, the images on the wall seemed to taunt her with frozen smiles, the faces circled in red grease pencil . . . Sam . . . Emma . . . Carolee . . .

All the dead girls. He'd circled all their faces. Plus one—one other face that Kirsten hadn't noticed before, circled bold and thick. She ripped it off the wall for a closer look. And in the first split-second of recognition, her mind's chaos rallied into a stubborn wall of denial, trying to convince herself that the face wasn't circled, because it made no sense for this face to be circled, only dead people were circled and the person inside the circle wasn't dead, was alive as . . . as . . .

. . . as she was.

It was her face.

Her own face marked like the others. Circled. Like a target.

Carolee . . . Sam . . . Emma . . . me, she thought. Marked for death. Like the last in a line of victims.

"No . . ." The sound welled up from deep within, hoarse and rasping. She clutched the photo to her chest, not wanting to let go of it, as if taking it away would prevent her own . . .

Her own what?

Murder.

Jeremy Iversen

21 The age at which freedom rings
The number of drinks consumed in one night

The honest new novel about the
greatest day in a college kid's life

PUBLISHED BY SIMON PULSE

feel the fear.

FEAR STREET® NIGHTS

A brand-new Fear Street trilogy by the master of horror

R.L. STINE

Coming in Summer 2005

Simon Pulse
Published by Simon & Schuster
FEAR STREET is a registered trademark of Parachute Press, Inc.

NEWLY WED

Nancy Krulik

The honeymoon just ended.
And Jesse and Jen are about to
get a hilarious helping of reality.

It's a year in the life of one young couple, two
opinionated best friends, and more meddling
family members than you can count.

This I swear.

PUBLISHED BY SIMON PULSE